Exactly Like My Father

Adult Children of Alcoholics, Family Trauma, and Finding Hope

Howard Kane

Hidden Alpha Capital LLC

About the author

Howard Kane writes the stories most people are afraid to tell.

As a former Fortune 500 executive, he knows what it feels like to appear successful on the outside while quietly unraveling on the inside. For years, he hid his drinking behind late nights, busy calendars, and a polished smile. When he finally faced the truth about his addiction, he discovered that recovery wasn't just possible; it was life-changing.

Howard channels that experience into memoir-style novels that explore addiction, family trauma, money, and power. His five-book saga, ***The Daughter of a Drunk***, follows Olivia Parker from a terrified little girl in a small Ohio town, vowing she'll never be like her father, to a woman fighting billionaires, corrupt institutions, and her own worst impulses. Beginning with ***Never Like My Father*** and ***Exactly Like My Father***, the series blends coming-of-age drama, generational alcoholism, and high-stakes whistleblower suspense into one continuous, bingeable story.

He also writes standalone novels rooted in alcohol dependence and recovery, including ***The Double Life of a High-Functioning Alcoholic***, which pulls back the curtain on the addiction that hides behind ambition and success, and ***From Wine Mom to Sober Mom***, which shines a light on the unique struggles mothers face when drinking threatens everything they love.

Through raw honesty and lived experience, Howard's books show that surviving a drunk parent or being the drunk parent is only the beginning. The real story is what you do with the wreckage. Readers describe his work as "impossible to put down" because the characters feel uncomfortably real, and their choices never come cheap.

If you've ever questioned your relationship with drinking, grown up in the shadow of someone else's, or wondered how far you'd go to protect the people you love, Howard Kane's stories are for you.

Website: https://selfcarejourneybooks.com/

Contents

Chapter One

The Promise that I Broke

"**L**EO'S DEAD."

The words slammed into me at 8:17 in the morning, right there in the corner booth at Grinders Cafe. The air was thick with roasted coffee beans and sticky-sweet cinnamon rolls. A highlighter slipped in my damp hand as I stared at the page of my economics book. Somewhere close, a laptop keyboard clicked in a steady rhythm, as if finals week was all that mattered.

Normal sounds. Normal smells. Then Mom's voice cut straight through it all.

"What do you mean, dead?"

My own voice didn't sound right. It was flat, cracked, like it belonged to somebody else. The highlighter slid from my fingers and tapped against the scarred table. That tiny sound felt too loud for a world that had just broken.

"They killed him!" Mom's words came jagged, torn apart. "Behind the warehouse. Oh God, there's so much blood."

The line hissed with static. My chest pounded so hard I could feel it in my throat, behind my eyes, flooding my ears until it swallowed the hiss of the espresso machine.

Then Uncle Mike's voice came through, low and worn: "Olivia. You need to come home. Now."

Silence.

I stared at my phone. At Chapter Twelve with its yellow streak bleeding across the page like a wound. The letters blurred, slid into each other, turned useless.

This isn't real.

The cafe's air pressed heavy, thick as wet wool. The cinnamon smell turned sour in my stomach. My skin went clammy, like the heat had drained from the room.

At the next table, a girl laughed at her screen. The sound scratched across my nerves like nails on glass. How could anyone laugh when the world had just split apart?

I gripped the table edge so hard my fingers burned. The wood was rough, sharp under my skin, the only solid thing holding me to Earth.

Leo can't be dead. Dead was for old men, for people with gray hair and hospital gowns. Not for my nineteen-year-old brother.

It felt like steel bands were tightening around my ribs with every breath.

"You okay?" The laughing girl was looking at me now, her words distant, muffled, as if she spoke from underwater.

"Fine," I rasped. "Just family stuff."

Family stuff. Careful, useless words for the end of the world.

I pushed up too fast. My chair screeched against the tile. My hands shook as I scooped up my books, clumsy, desperate to pretend I could still move like everything was normal.

The walk back to my dorm stretched on forever. Each step dragged, heavy, like wading through sand. A car horn blasted when I stepped into the crosswalk without looking, and the jolt sent my textbook slipping from my arms.

On my narrow dorm bed, the springs groaned under me. My phone buzzed again, angry against my palm. Unknown number. Millfield area code.

This has to be the call. Someone to explain the mistake. A doctor saying Leo made it to the hospital. A cop saying unconscious but breathing. Something. Anything.

Two missed calls. A voicemail waiting. I couldn't hit play. Not yet. Because once I listened, it would mean no mistake at all.

The drive from Columbus to Millfield was ninety-seven minutes. Each one felt endless.

Mile after mile, I strangled the steering wheel until my knuckles turned white. The radio spit out some bouncy pop song that felt like an insult in the silence of my new life.

The GPS voice pulled me down streets I knew too well. Past the high school where Leo had dropped out. Past Morrison's Grocery, where I bagged groceries to help keep the lights on. Past Maple Street, where the curtains still sagged in our old windows and Mom lived alone.

The police station looked the same as when Dad got booked for DUIs. Brick, narrow windows, the smell of disinfectant stretched too thin to hide what lingered beneath.

But walking inside ripped away the last of my denial.

A TV mounted in the corner played the local news on mute. Something about Carrington Media acquiring another newspaper. The ticker read: "Media Empire Expands Midwest Presence."

Mom sat crumpled in a chair, Uncle Mike's arm around her like it might hold her together. She looked up when I came in, and I saw something in her eyes that made my stomach cave. Not sadness. Not anger. Just… gone. Like the last thread holding her to hope had finally snapped.

"Olivia." She said my name like it was a prayer God never bothered to hear. "I'm so sorry. I'm so sorry you have to see this."

Sorry I had to see it. As if Leo's death wasn't mine to carry too. As if it wasn't my fault for choosing grades over family.

Detective Doyle was younger than I expected, early thirties maybe, with a heavy face that said he'd seen this before. He led me into a small interview room that reeked of stale coffee and failure.

"I'm sorry for your loss," he said, sitting across from me. "I know this is hard, but I need to ask about your brother's recent activities."

"What happened?" My voice snapped, sharper than I meant. "My mom said he was shot, but I don't—"

"Leo was found this morning behind the warehouse on Fifth Street. Single gunshot wound to the head. Execution-style. We believe it was connected to a drug debt."

Execution-style. The words cracked across me like a whip. Someone put a gun to my baby brother's head. Someone pulled the trigger.

"How much?" My voice shook.

He frowned. "How much what?"

"How much did he owe them?"

Detective Doyle flipped through his notes, his pen tapping softly. "From what we can gather, about eight thousand dollars. Started small. With interest and penalties, it grew fast."

Doyle's pen tapped against his notepad. "These aren't your typical street dealers. The operation we're looking at... it's more sophisticated than we first thought."

Eight thousand dollars. The exact number glowing in my checking account. My summer internship money. The money I'd been guarding for Chicago. Deposits, interview suits, the first steps of a life I thought was solid.

"When did you last speak with your brother?" he asked. Something cold slid down my spine.

The truth was a knot I couldn't untangle for this stranger. How could I explain that Leo had reached out and I'd pushed him to voicemail because thesis deadlines and job interviews mattered more?

"A few weeks ago," I said, my voice careful, small. "He was having some troubles. I told him I'd help with treatment but not with anything else."

"How did he respond to that?"

I closed my eyes. Saw Leo's face the last time we'd been in the same room. Saw the flicker of fear when he realized I'd chosen my perfect life over him.

"He wasn't happy," I admitted.

"Did he try to contact you after that?"

My throat tightened. "He called a few times. I was busy with finals and thesis work, so I didn't always answer."

Detective Doyle scribbled something down.

The rest of the interview blurred. When Doyle finally led me back to the waiting area, Mom and Uncle Mike were still there, frozen in the same chairs, bent under a weight too heavy for anybody.

"Olivia." Mom's fingers found mine, cold and trembling. "I need to ask you something, and I need you to be honest."

I braced myself.

"Did you know how bad it was? Did you know he was in real danger?"

The truth was more tangled than she could bear. Leo had told me he was in trouble, but I'd thought it was another storm tough love could weather. I'd thought not enabling him was the right thing.

"He told me he owed money to dangerous people," I said softly. "But I thought helping him pay would just feed the habit."

Mom's face folded in on itself. "Eight thousand dollars," she whispered. "He died over eight thousand dollars, and you had that money."

It wasn't a question. It was a verdict that hung between us.

The drive back to Columbus felt like I was inside someone else's life.

I kept my hands at ten and two. Eyes forward. Slow, steady breaths. All the moves of a person who was fine. A person who had it together. A person who did not just hear that her brother was murdered while she was coloring over economics formulas.

The highway stretched out in front of me. Gray road into gray sky. Everything looked like ash.

My phone sat in the cup holder. Quiet now. But I could still hear Mom. They killed him. Behind the warehouse. Oh God, there is so much blood.

I turned up the radio. A pop song about summer and beaches and being in love. A song for people whose brothers were still alive.

Back in my dorm, my desk was still covered with the morning's life: thesis outline, McKinsey paperwork, the bones of my careful future. All of it meaningless now.

Sometime after midnight, my thoughts drifted to another promise. One made years ago, kneeling by Dad's hospital bed while machines beeped down his last hours. His hand had been weak but insistent, gripping mine.

"Promise me," he'd whispered. "Promise me you'll take care of Mom and Leo."

And I'd promised. I'd looked him in the eyes and promised I'd be the one who stayed, who didn't abandon the people who needed me.

But when Leo needed me most, when his life was balanced on a knife's edge, I chose my resume over his survival.

Eight thousand dollars. Less than my McKinsey signing bonus. Less than I'd spent on textbooks over four years.

My brother had died for what would soon be pocket change in my new life.

I finally drifted into sleep around three a.m. In my dream, Leo was seven again, building pillow forts in the living room while Dad raged in the kitchen. He looked at me with total trust and said, "You'll always protect me, right Livvy? No matter what?"

And dream-me said yes, the way real-me had said yes a dozen times growing up.

But when I woke up, Leo was still dead. And I was still the sister who'd broken the most sacred promise she'd ever made.

I needed to understand how I got here. How the sister who spent eighteen years protecting Leo became the sister who did not save him.

So I went back. Three months. To January, when everything still felt perfect.

Chapter Two

The Calls I Ignored

THREE MONTHS AGO, JANUARY in Columbus hit like a slap.

I woke at 5:17 a.m. Same time as always for four years. My heart raced before my eyes opened. Sheets damp with fear sweat I made in my sleep.

The nightmares were worse. Dad throwing plates at the wall. Leo pressed against the back of my legs. The smell of whiskey and broken glass. The drowning feeling.

My therapist called it trauma. Old leftovers. Not a sign of my future.

I got out of bed. My jaw ached from grinding all night. My back hurt from sleeping straight as a board.

Outside, the cold burned my nose and watered my eyes. I barely felt it. My heart pounded so hard it drowned out everything else.

McKinsey was sending interview decisions that day.

I checked my phone every thirty seconds. My thumb hurt from swiping. My stomach rolled every time I pictured my inbox.

The lecture hall smelled like old coffee and floor wax. I slipped inside and found a corner. My fingers shook while I unlocked my phone.

One new email.

McKinsey & Company: Interview Decision.

My vision went fuzzy. I blinked until the words came back.

Congratulations, Ms. Parker. We are pleased to invite you to our final round of interviews at our Chicago office...

The sound that left my mouth was part sob and part scream.

Two students by the vending machine stared. One looked scared, like I might fall apart.

I was not falling apart.

I was breaking through.

McKinsey wanted me. The top firm wanted Olivia Parker from nowhere, Ohio. The girl whose dad drowned himself in whiskey. The girl whose brother shot poison into his veins.

They wanted me.

My legs turned to water. I leaned into the cold concrete wall. It felt solid against my back.

This was proof. Real proof. The promise I made on that bathroom floor at six years old had done something.

I had been running from Dad's ghost for eighteen years.

Now I had evidence. I had outrun him.

The next three weeks were brutal.

I studied until my eyes burned and my back ached from the chair that never fit my body. Third floor of the library. Northeast corner. Table against the wall so I could see every entrance.

The carpet up there was an ugly brown, made to hide stains. It smelled like old paper and industrial cleaner.

I had taken that seat for four years. Back to the wall. Eyes on the exits.

My therapist said I studied like a soldier waiting for an attack.

She was right. She did not understand. When your dad throws dinner plates and your brother goes missing for days, you learn to watch doors. You learn to listen for the smallest sound.

That watching kept me alive.

On the morning of my Chicago interview, I woke at 4 a.m. and threw up from nerves.

The train ride felt endless. I pressed my forehead to the window and watched Ohio fields slide by. My stomach churned. The coffee I bought tasted awful, but I drank it anyway.

McKinsey's offices filled four floors of a glass tower downtown.

Marble floors that echoed underfoot. Abstract art that cost more than Dad's house. The air smelled like expensive cologne and fresh flowers.

I arrived thirty minutes early. I watched the people who worked there.

Men in perfect suits. Women in fitted dresses, heels clicking across the marble. Leather briefcases that looked handmade.

These were going to be my people. Smart. Steady. Fixers. The kind who solved problems instead of making them.

The kind who never had to choose between their future and their family's survival.

The interview took three hours.

Case studies about market expansion. About operations. My throat went dry from talking, but I kept going. I walked through my logic, step by step.

My palms were sweaty as I did math on the whiteboard. Every answer landed.

Almost.

Halfway through the second case, my mind froze. It was like running into a wall.

The senior manager, Jennifer Walsh, watched me. She waited. Her expression was kind, then a little worried.

Numbers swam on the board. My heart slammed against my ribs.

You are going to fail. Just like Dad said. Just like everyone back home knows.

The voice in my head sounded like Dad after too many drinks.

My hand shook. The marker slipped in my sweaty grip. A thin stream of sweat ran down my spine.

"Take your time," Jennifer said.

But time was the trap. Every second I stood silent was proof I did not belong. Proof that Olivia Parker from Millfield could not keep up with kids from Yale, Harvard, and Stanford.

I closed my eyes. I breathed. I pushed the panic down as far as it would go.

I started over from the beginning. Slower this time. Each step was deliberate.

The answer came.

"Excellent recovery," Jennifer said when I finally finished. "That's exactly the kind of composure we look for."

I nodded, but my hands still shook as we moved on to the next case.

Three days later, the offer letter arrived.

I was in my corner of the library, the same spot I always claimed. Someone nearby typed on their laptop, that steady click like rain on a roof.

Subject line: "Offer Letter: Confidential." From Jennifer Walsh.

My hands trembled as I opened it.

Starting salary: $150,000. Signing bonus: $25,000.

I read it three times before it sank in.

My heart pounded in my ears, in my throat, behind my eyes.

This was real.

I had escaped. For real this time. The pull of the Parker family mess couldn't drag me back. Not anymore.

The celebration dinner happened three weeks later.

Professor Williams chose a fancy place downtown. Cloth napkins felt soft against my fingers. Wine lists were printed on heavy paper that rustled like money.

The whole place smelled like garlic, warm bread, and something expensive I couldn't name.

We sat by the window. City lights shimmered in the glass like stars floating on black water.

"To Olivia." Professor Williams raised his glass, deep red wine catching the light. "Who proved that exceptional students do, in fact, find exceptional opportunities."

I lifted my water glass. Always water. Never alcohol.

That bathroom floor promise was the only one I'd kept.

Five other seniors crowded the table, all bound for consulting, finance, and law. For two hours, we swapped stories about apartments in Chicago, bonuses, and office gossip about firms that already felt like ours.

This was the life I'd built. Controlled. Safe. Surrounded by people who solved problems instead of creating them.

My phone buzzed as dessert landed on the table: a chocolate mountain so rich it tasted like eating straight frosting.

The screen lit up: Leo.

My stomach twisted. That familiar punch, family chaos showing up to interrupt my carefully staged success.

But this was my night. My proof. My victory.

Whatever Leo needed could wait an hour.

I sent the call to voicemail, slid my phone face-down on the table, and turned back to the laughter and the talk of city apartments.

The irony would take months to gut me. While I chewed on expensive chocolate and toasted to my escape, my brother was making a desperate call to the only person who might have saved him.

The next morning, I walked back from Economics of Labor Markets, still high on the glow of everything falling into place.

The Chicago interview had been nearly flawless. The one moment of panic? Erased by recovery. The offer was signed. My life laid out like a golden road.

Graduation. Chicago. Six figures. Everything I'd been clawing toward since I was six.

My phone buzzed.

Text from Leo: Can I come visit this weekend? Really need to talk to you.

I was crossing the quad. Students were throwing Frisbees, sprawled on blankets, laughing even though it was still February in Ohio.

I typed back: Super busy with thesis stuff. Maybe in a few weeks?

What I didn't write: I was too busy being the golden girl to deal with another family storm.

What I didn't know: Leo hadn't slept in three days. He was hiding in Mom's basement, flinching every time a car slowed outside.

I slid my phone back into my pocket. Study group for Corporate Finance, then thesis, then the honors society meeting.

My days stacked in neat fifteen-minute blocks, each one building the perfect résumé that would carry me away from all of this.

Three days later, someone pounded on my dorm room door.

Not knocking. Pounding. The sound of someone using their whole fist.

Sarah was at her boyfriend's, so it was just me and my thesis.

I opened the door.

Leo stood there.

He looked awful. Worse than awful. His face was hollow, eyes sunken deep. His clothes sagged on him, as if his body had melted inside them.

But his hands scared me most. Shaking so hard, he stuffed them into his jacket pockets to keep them still.

"Livvy." His voice cracked. "Thank God you're here."

"Leo? What are you... I told you I was busy—"

"I need to come in. Please. I can't be out here."

He pushed past me before I could answer.

The smell hit me first. Three days of no shower. Cigarettes. That sharp, chemical tang I remembered from Dad's worst binges.

My perfect dorm room felt tainted. My tidy stacks of research. My clean sheets. My thesis printout with crisp margins. All of it invaded.

"Leo, you can't just show up like this—"

"I did call. I texted. You said you were too busy." His eyes flicked to the window, then the door, then back to me. Wild, cornered. "Livvy, I'm in real trouble this time. Life-threatening trouble."

Life-threatening.

The phrase Dad had used too, every time he wanted money. Every emergency was life-threatening until the cash came through. Then it was just another Monday.

"What kind of trouble?" I asked, already working out how to get him out before Sarah returned.

"Cocaine," he said, his body trembling in rhythm with his voice. "I owe these guys... a lot of money."

He dropped into my desk chair. The one I'd bought with summer internship money.

"How much?"

"Started at two grand. But there's interest. Daily interest. Penalties. It's up to eight now."

Eight thousand.

I had $8,247 sitting in my account.

"They're not patient people, Livvy." His voice shook as much as his hands. "They beat up two others who couldn't pay. Put one in the hospital."

My throat closed. Eight thousand was everything I had. The seed money for Chicago. The cushion that was supposed to carry me into my new life.

"I'll help you," I said. "But not like that."

"What do you mean?"

"I'll pay for real treatment. Rehab. Somewhere residential. But I'm not handing money to drug dealers."

His face collapsed, like I'd slapped him.

"Livvy, these aren't people who care about my recovery timeline. They want their money. Now. Or they'll—" He stopped, swallowed hard. "Please. I'm begging you."

I folded my arms across my chest, creating a wall between us.

"Maybe you should have thought about that before getting mixed up with them."

The words came out sharp, colder than I intended.

But wasn't I right? I'd read the articles. Taken psychology classes. Every lecture, every handout said the same thing: Don't give addicts money. It makes the disease worse.

"You remember that game we played?" His voice softened, almost childlike. "When Dad was drunk? We'd hide in the basement. Hold hands. You told me as long as we stayed together, we'd be safe."

I remembered. Of course, I remembered.

"We're adults now, Leo," I said. "I can't keep fixing your problems."

Something flickered in his eyes. Some last spark of trust in me.

He pushed himself up, shoulders slumped, and walked to the door.

"I hope Chicago is everything you want," he said.

His hand was on the knob when I blurted, "Get clean, Leo. Really clean. And I'll help. With school. With starting fresh. All of it."

He turned just enough for me to see his face. "And if I'm dead by then?"

"Don't be dramatic."

"I'm not being dramatic, Livvy. I'm being realistic."

The door clicked shut.

Silence pressed in. My room was spotless again, but the air felt wrong. I stared at the empty chair he'd left behind, the cushion still warm.

I should go after him. Call him back. Do something.

Instead, I grabbed the Febreze. Sprayed until the air smelled fake and clean. Sat down. Opened my thesis file. Fifty pages to review before my advisor meeting.

That was the last time I ever saw my brother alive.

Over the next six weeks, he called fourteen times.

I answered twice.

The first was three days after he came. I was in the library, slipped into the stairwell with his voice buzzing through the line.

"Livvy, thank God. Look, I've been thinking. About treatment. Maybe you're right—"

"That's great, Leo. I can help research programs. Cleveland has some solid places—"

"But I need to deal with this debt first. I can't check into rehab with these guys after me. They'll find me there."

And there it was. The hook. The same loop every time. Rehab was impossible without money. Money I refused to give.

"Then talk to the police," I said.

"The police?" He barked a laugh, bitter and raw. "Livvy, you don't call cops on these people. That's how you end up in the hospital. Or worse."

"Then maybe you shouldn't have gotten involved in the first place."

Silence. Just the sound of his breath, shaky and uneven.

"Yeah," he said at last. "Maybe I shouldn't have."

He hung up.

The second time came two weeks later. I was walking to Business Ethics when his name flashed across my screen. The irony stung.

"Leo?"

"Livvy." His voice was small, stripped of all the usual bluster. "I'm hiding in an abandoned building on the east side. They know where Mom lives now. They've been watching the house."

My chest seized.

"What do you mean, watching?"

"Driving by slowly. Parking out front. Yesterday one of them knocked. Asked for me. Mom told them I wasn't there, but—"

"But what?"

"They said they'll keep checking. Real polite. Said they know I'll come home eventually."

I stopped walking. Students brushed past, laughing, heading to class. Normal lives. Normal problems.

"Leo, come stay with me. We'll figure it out."

"I can't. They're following me. I can't bring this to your dorm, not with graduation so close."

"Where are you sleeping?"

"Abandoned building. McDonald's when I need food. My phone's dying."

I wanted to save him. I did. But every path circled back to the same demand. Money.

And I couldn't do it. I couldn't risk enabling him.

So I held the line.

Mom called too. Six times. I answered three.

"Leo looks terrified," she said once. "He's nineteen years old and hiding like a fugitive."

"He needs to face consequences," I told her. "That's the only way he'll learn."

"This isn't about lessons anymore."

"What do you expect? For me to quit school and chase his mess?"

"I want you to remember he's your brother."

"And I want him to remember choices have consequences."

I was so sure I was right. Tough love. Boundaries. That's what every article preached. Every psychology class confirmed.

What I didn't know? Some situations blow past textbooks. Some require action now, not later.

What I didn't know? My brother was going to die while I waited for him to "learn."

The last call came at 2:47 a.m. on April 15.

Three nights before everything ended.

I was asleep when my phone lit up. I saw his name. Half-awake, I pressed decline. I rolled over.

When I woke up, two texts waited.

3:15 a.m.: They found me. I love you, sis. I'm sorry I couldn't be strong like you.

3:18 a.m.: I recorded this message seven times before I got the courage to send it. My hands are shaking so hard I can barely type. I'm proud of you, Livvy. Remember that drawing I made when I was eight? The one of us as stick figures holding hands? I still believe we could be like that again if I got clean. I love you. I'm sorry I was such a disappointment.

I read them while brushing my teeth, toothpaste foam in my mouth.

My first thought wasn't panic; it was annoyance.

Leo being dramatic again. Leo using guilt when I was days from defending my thesis.

I spit into the sink. I deleted both texts. I didn't respond.

I got dressed. I went to class.

Just another day. Three days later, Mom called.

Leo was dead.

And I realized the texts I deleted were his last words. That while I slept safe in my dorm bed, rolling my eyes at his "drama," he was bleeding out behind a warehouse, calling for me until his voice went quiet.

The pact we made as kids, to keep each other safe, had twisted into the betrayal that killed him.

I'd built walls to keep the chaos out. I forgot walls also keep love from getting in. By the time I learned the difference, it was too late.

Leo died believing his big sister would come, and I lived believing I was right to let him fall.

Chapter Three

Blood on Concrete

Uncle Mike's car smelled like old coffee, worn leather, and the pine tree air freshener swinging from the rearview. I pressed my cheek against the icy window and watched Ohio blur past in strips of gray and brown.

Linda had stopped crying about an hour ago. Now she just stared straight ahead, her eyes swollen and glassy, blinking too infrequently. In her lap, a shredded tissue kept falling apart, little white scraps piling like snow.

"How much farther?" I asked, though I didn't want the answer.

"Twenty minutes," Uncle Mike said, his voice rough, gravel caught in his throat. "Maybe less."

I looked at him through the mirror. His eyes had aged ten years in three days. Grief does that and carves out lines you didn't have before.

The closer we got to Cleveland, the harder it was to pretend. This was real. Leo was gone. We were driving to see his body. This was happening to us, to our family, to my world that was supposed to keep him safe.

My stomach twisted, car sick in a way that went deeper than motion. It was the sickness of forever change. The kind that had no cure.

The Cleveland morgue looked exactly like the kind of place that held the dead.

Gray concrete walls. Windows too narrow to let in real light. The parking lot smelled of exhaust and something sharper, chemical and cold.

Uncle Mike held the door open. The smell inside hit like a slap. Disinfectant layered over floor cleaner, with something beneath that couldn't be scrubbed away.

It was the smell of endings.

The hallway stretched on forever. Our footsteps cracked against the tile like gunshots. Linda's breathing grew louder with every step, jagged inhales that made me think she'd crumble before we reached the room.

This can't be right, I kept thinking. Leo can't actually be here, waiting on a table behind some door.

But I knew it was right. The call had been too steady. Doyle had been too calm. The blood at the warehouse too red to belong to anyone else.

The woman at the desk looked worn in a way that went beyond tired. Her face said she'd watched grief walk through too many doors. Her eyes were flat, emptied out.

"Parker family?" she asked, not looking up from her clipboard.

"Yes," Uncle Mike said. His voice scraped raw.

"I'm sorry for your loss. If you'll follow me."

The viewing room was so cold it burned my lungs. The air carried that sharp chemical bite that stuck in the back of my throat. Fluorescent lights buzzed overhead, harsh and angry, throwing a bright glare and dark shadows into every corner.

My teeth began to chatter, not from the cold but from fear.

Three metal tables sat in the room. Two gleamed empty. One was draped with a white sheet.

The shape underneath was too still. Too small.

My knees buckled. Uncle Mike's hand clamped around my elbow, digging in hard enough to bruise. The pain barely registered.

"Linda, maybe you should wait outside," he whispered, his voice breaking.

"No." She straightened, her shoulders stiff. "I need to see him. I need to see my baby."

The medical examiner was a woman with kind eyes and steady hands. She had the look of someone who'd spent years learning how to remain gentle in cruel places.

"Are you ready?" she asked.

We weren't. Not even close. But we nodded anyway.

She pulled back the sheet.

And there was Leo.

My little brother. Right there. As real as anything.

But not real at all.

His skin was gray-white, the color of old wax. His lips were a purple-blue. His eyes were shut tight, not like sleeping but as if the light inside had been switched off for good.

His sandy hair still stuck up in that stubborn cowlick on the left. Someone had tried to press it down, but it sprang back anyway. Even in death, his hair wouldn't behave. That stupid cowlick broke me more than anything. So ordinary. So him.

Linda made a sound I'd never heard before. Not a scream, not a sob. Just raw grief breaking loose.

Her legs gave way. Not dramatically like in the movies. Just a sudden collapse, strength gone. Uncle Mike caught her, grunting under the weight.

"My baby," she whispered, her voice wet and shattered. "My beautiful baby."

Her hand reached for Leo's face, then snapped back like the cold burned.

"He's so cold, Mike. He's so cold."

I couldn't cry. Couldn't move. Couldn't do anything but stare at his hands.

They'd been folded across his chest, as if to make him look peaceful. But I could see the dirt under his nails, the scrapes across his knuckles.

Those were the same hands that once held mine tight while we hid from Dad's rages in the basement. The same hands that texted me stupid jokes, crooked drawings, and pleas for help.

Now they were just hands. Cold. Stiff. Never going to reach for anything again.

"He looks peaceful," the examiner said softly.

But it was a lie.

He didn't look peaceful. He looked empty. Like someone had scooped out everything that made him Leo (his laugh, his ridiculous hope) and left this shell behind.

Just a body. That's all this was now. A body that used to be my brother.

"Can we have a moment?" Uncle Mike asked, his voice thick.

The examiner nodded, her shoes squeaking softly as she slipped away, leaving us alone.

Linda hovered, her hand trembling inches above his face, too afraid to touch.

"I carried him inside me for nine months," she whispered. "Felt every kick. Every hiccup. I knew his heartbeat before I knew his face." Her hand fell back to her lap. "And now he's just... gone. Just gone."

I wanted to touch him too. Shake him awake. Tell him this was a mistake, that he could stop pretending, that we could all go home.

But my arms stayed heavy at my sides, like concrete.

Because this was real. The metal table. The smell. The waxy skin. The still chest.

My little brother was dead.

The lights buzzed above us. The hallway echoed faintly. Linda's gasps tore through the silence.

And Leo lay cold, still, nineteen forever.

I stood over him and finally felt the weight of what I had done.

Detective Doyle was waiting when we came out.

He looked like a man who'd walked this hallway too many times, seen too many families come apart in morgues. He knew the weight of grief, how heavy it pressed down.

"I'm sorry you had to go through that," he said. His feet shifted, his eyes dodging mine. "Look, I... there's some additional information from the investigation."

He stopped. Cleared his throat. Started again, then froze.

"What is it?" Linda asked.

He rubbed the back of his neck. "Maybe we should wait. You've been through enough."

"Just tell us," I said.

"I don't think—" His eyes flicked to Uncle Mike, like he was asking permission to stay quiet. "It won't change anything. Maybe it's better if—"

"Tell us." My voice was sharper than I intended.

He sighed, pulled out his notebook, but kept it closed in his hands, like even opening it was dangerous.

"We've been interviewing witnesses near where Leo was found. Several people saw him in the past few days." He paused again. "You sure you want to hear this?"

I nodded, even though my stomach was already knotting.

"He was hiding in an abandoned building about six blocks from the warehouse," Doyle said slowly, each word measured, like stepping through a minefield. "According to witnesses, Leo…"

He looked directly at me then. There was pity in his eyes.

"He what?" Linda's voice cracked.

"He kept talking about his sister," Doyle said softly, almost like an apology. "He told people his sister would pay his debt."

The air vanished from my lungs.

"Detective," Uncle Mike said. "That's enough."

"There's more," Doyle said. His tone suggested he hated every word. "I'm sorry, but you should know. One man said Leo showed him a piece of paper with a phone number written on it."

Doyle's eyes remained locked on me. Regret weighed heavily in them.

"Your number, Miss Parker. He carried it in his pocket. Said it made him feel safe."

My number. In his pocket. As if it could protect him.

Doyle's jaw tightened. "I probably shouldn't tell you this next part. It won't help."

"Please," I whispered.

He closed his eyes for a moment, then opened them again, heavy with reluctance.

"He told people around him, 'My sister will pay. She's got the money. She loves me.'"

The words hit like bullets, each one landing cleanly.

I stared at him, but his voice became muffled, like I was hearing through water.

She loves me.

Leo had died believing that. Bleeding out on concrete, still trusting that his big sister loved him enough to save him.

And I'd shown him my love came with conditions. With deadlines he couldn't meet.

The hallway tilted. The lights glared too bright. My body swayed though my feet remained planted.

"I shouldn't have told you that," Doyle said quickly. "It's not your fault. What I mean is—"

But something cracked open inside me. Whatever had been holding tight since I'd seen Leo's waxy face finally split.

I started sobbing. Not movie-pretty tears. The real kind: snot, gasps, sounds that tore out of me like an animal in pain.

"Miss Parker," Doyle said gently. "This wasn't your fault. You couldn't have known—"

"I did know," I choked. "He called. He texted. He told me."

Doyle flinched. "I'm sorry. I thought... I thought you'd want to know he wasn't alone. That he had hope."

Hope. He'd died with hope because I'd taught him his big sister would always show up. Until I didn't.

"He died still believing in you," Doyle said quietly. "If that helps."

But it didn't help. It gutted me. Because it meant Leo's last thought wasn't anger. It was trust. And that trust had been wasted.

Doyle drove us to the crime scene because Linda said she needed to see it.

I didn't want to go. Didn't want to stand where my brother begged for his life while I was annoyed at his messages in my dorm room.

But you don't get to choose what you see once you've killed someone.

The warehouse on Fifth Street sat in a row of abandoned buildings. Some had faded "Club Vertical - Opening 2015" banners still hanging on the chain-link fences. This whole district had been left to rot after a failed development deal years ago.

The air stank of rust, old oil, and something sour that hinted at decay.

The April wind cut through my jacket and raised goose-bumps on my arms. Or maybe that was just fear.

Behind the warehouse on Fifth Street, yellow police tape flapped and snapped in the wind. The sound was sharp. Ac-cusing.

"He was found right here," Doyle said.

He pointed to a dark stain on the ground. Three feet wide. Blood. Leo's blood.

It had dried to the color of rust. Old pennies left to weather. The edges black, the middle faded pale under days of sun.

My brother's life soaked into the dirty concrete.

Linda made that sound again. That awful choking noise, like she was drowning even though there was no water. Her whole body shook with it.

"The medical examiner said it would have been quick," Detective Doyle offered, his voice soft. "He wouldn't have suffered long."

Wouldn't have suffered long. Like if that fixed anything. Like terror didn't count if it only lasted seconds.

My legs moved on their own. I walked to the stain. Knelt down beside it.

The concrete scraped my knees. Cold. Gritty. I swore I could still smell something metallic in the air, even though the blood had dried days ago. Maybe it was real. Maybe it was just in my head.

This was where Leo died. Right here. This exact spot. Where the bullet landed. Where he fell. Where he called for me until nineteen years of life collapsed into a dark patch that rain would wash away.

"His phone was found about ten feet away," Doyle said, pointing toward the wall. "The screen cracked when it hit the ground, but it still worked."

He paused, his throat tight.

"There were texts. Final messages. To your number."

The words slammed into me.

"I need to see them," I said. My voice didn't sound like mine. Flat. Mechanical.

"Olivia—" Uncle Mike started.

"I need to see them."

Doyle pulled out his phone. Hesitated. Then began reading.

"'They found me. I love you, sis. I'm sorry I couldn't be strong like you.' Sent at 3:15 a.m."

Every word sliced through me.

"And then at 3:18: 'I recorded this message seven times before I got the courage to send it. My hands are shaking so hard I can barely type. I'm proud of you, Livvy. Remember that drawing I made when I was eight? The one of us as stick figures holding hands? I still believe we could be like that again if I got clean. I love you. I'm sorry I was such a disappointment.'"

Relief and devastation crashed into each other inside me.

I had seen those texts. Read them while brushing my teeth. Deleted them like junk mail. My brother's last words. Annoyance had been my only response.

Linda was circling the lot in slow, searching loops. Her eyes combed the ground as if she could find pieces of him the police had missed. Some clue that would make it make sense.

Her shoes scraped against the concrete, the sound echoing off the empty warehouse walls.

I walked away from the stain. Away from Linda's circling. Away from Doyle's pity.

I stopped at the chain-link fence at the edge of the lot. Gripped the metal until my knuckles turned white. The fence rattled in the wind. Hollow. Empty.

Detective Doyle followed me a few steps, then stopped. He looked around the empty lot like he was checking for witnesses. When he spoke again, his voice was different. Lower. Careful.

"Miss Parker." He shifted his weight, uncomfortable. "There's something else. Between you and me... we're seeing patterns. A similar execution several days before Leo died at the same location."

I turned to look at him.

"Someone's consolidating power," he continued, his voice barely above a whisper. "And they have protection. High up. This isn't just about local dealers."

He glanced back at Linda, still searching the ground, then back to me.

"Your brother might have been caught up in something bigger than any of us realized."

"What do you mean?" I asked.

"We are still investigating the details, but just... be careful."

The ride back to Millfield was quiet except for Linda's crying. Her gasps filled the car, jagged and endless. I stared out the window. Same gray sky. Same bare trees. But they didn't look the same anymore. They looked like the world where Leo was supposed to live. Grow up. Get married. Have kids. Grow old.

All those futures gone. Left behind on concrete.

When we got home, I went straight to my room and opened my laptop. I logged into my bank account. The number glowed on the screen, one I already knew by heart: $8,247.

Eight thousand, two hundred forty-seven dollars. More money than Leo needed. Enough to buy his life back. More than most people saw in months.

I clicked over to my McKinsey offer letter.

Starting salary: $150,000. Signing bonus: $25,000. First-year comp: $175,000.

Leo had died for eight thousand. I was about to make twenty-two times that for putting my name on paper.

The math was so simple it felt obscene. His life was worth three weeks of my future salary. Less than one month of my bonus. Coffee money in the budget I'd written for myself.

I'd let my brother get executed over pocket change.

My thesis sat on the desk. Forty-seven pages, formatted and neat. Economic analysis I had decided mattered more than his life. Market theory over market reality. Reality that says people die when no one pays their debts.

The McKinsey business cards I'd ordered were stacked in a tidy pile: "Olivia Parker, Analyst." Proof I was different. Proof I was better.

But what kind of smart person lets her brother die with money just sitting in her checking account?

I don't know how long I sat there staring at the screens. Long enough for Linda's crying to fade downstairs, for Uncle Mike to leave, and for the house to sink into that thick, heavy silence that only comes after death.

Finally, I closed the laptop and went downstairs. Linda was at the kitchen table, hands wrapped around a coffee gone cold.

"I could have saved him," I said.

She looked up. Her eyes were red and hollow. Older than they'd been that morning.

"I know," she said.

"I had the money."

"I know."

We sat there in the silence after everything had ended. The silence where you realize love isn't always enough. That sometimes people die because you're too selfish to save them.

"What happens now?" I asked.

"I don't know," Linda said. "I buried your father. Now I bury your brother. I don't know what comes after that."

I wanted to say sorry. I wanted to promise I'd do better. I wanted to find words that could bring Leo back or at least soften the way Linda looked at me as if I wasn't hers anymore.

But sorry doesn't raise the dead. And promises from someone who has already broken the most important one are as worthless as dried blood on concrete.

So I said, "I need to go for a drive."

Linda nodded. She probably knew I wasn't coming back tonight. Maybe she knew I wasn't coming back at all.

I ended up at Murphy's without planning to. I just drove around in the dark until my headlights swept across the old sign.

Murphy's Tavern. Dad's favorite place to drink away rent money and groceries.

The door stuck when I pushed it. Same scrape against the concrete floor I remembered from when Mom sent me to drag Dad home for dinner.

Inside smelled exactly the same. Stale beer baked into wood. Cigarette smoke soaked into the walls. Fried food, Pine-Sol, and something sour underneath it all. The smell of promises broken so many times they rotted.

A few regulars hunched at the bar. Men I recognized were older now, but the same faces that used to lean against Dad. They didn't look up.

The bartender was younger than the old guy Dad knew, but his eyes were the same. Tired. Worn. Like he'd watched every kind of human misery cross that threshold.

I slid onto Dad's stool. Third from the end. Close to the bathroom. Far enough from the door that Linda couldn't see me from the lot when she came looking.

The vinyl cushion was cracked, patched with duct tape. It crinkled under me.

Behind the bar, bottles lined up in front of a cloudy mirror. Cheap whiskey. Bottom-shelf vodka. Plastic jugs of box wine. All the ways to make the noise stop.

"What can I get you?" the bartender asked.

I had never ordered alcohol in my life. Never even thought about it. The promise I'd made on a bathroom floor at six years old was the one thing that had held through many years of chaos.

But here I was, sitting in Dad's spot, about to make Dad's choice.

"Glass of wine," I heard myself say. "Red."

The bartender didn't ask which kind. He reached for one of the jugs without looking. There was only one kind here. The cheap kind. The kind that came in boxes and tasted like regret.

He poured it into a cloudy glass. The wine sloshed dark red, thick as blood that had been left sitting too long.

My hands shook as I picked it up.

This was it. The thing that killed Dad one sip at a time until nothing was left but a yellow-skinned body on a bathroom floor.

This was the enemy I'd spent my whole life running from.

But what was so powerful about it? What made it worth dying for? What made grown men trade their families for this?

I lifted the glass to my nose.

The smell hit like a slap. Sharp. Sour. Chemical. Nothing like the glossy wine commercials. This smelled like fermentation gone bad. Like sadness bottled for six bucks.

It smelled exactly like Dad's breath on the bad nights.

Six-year-old Olivia's voice cut through my head, clear as glass: "Dear God, I will never, ever, EVER be like my father."

My entire life sober and being the different one. My entire life proving I was stronger than the disease that killed Dad and dragged Leo under.

I'd built my whole identity on that promise. On being the Parker who didn't drink. The one who escaped.

But what's the point of escaping if everyone you love dies behind you? What's the point of being strong if strength means letting them go? What's the point of being different if different means alone?

I tilted the glass and let the wine touch my lips.

It tasted like betrayal. Like the sobriety promises dissolving on my tongue. Like the exact moment everything you built yourself on turns to dust.

The wine was warm and sour. It coated my mouth with a thickness that made me want to gag.

But beneath the awfulness was something else. Something whispering in Dad's voice: This could make it stop hurting.

One of the regulars coughed. Wet, rattling. The same cough Dad had toward the end.

I looked at myself in the cloudy mirror behind the bar. My face warped, distorted. As if I were already becoming someone else.

As if I were becoming Dad.

I set the glass down without taking another sip.

Not because I was strong. Not because the promise still held. But because I wasn't ready yet. Not ready to know what had lured Dad back here night after night. Not ready to find out if the same poison that killed him lived inside me too.

I pushed the glass away. Wine sloshed over the rim, sticky on the bar.

"You okay?" the bartender asked.

I nodded. Stood up. My legs wobbled. The stool scraped across the floor, the same sound Dad's had made a thousand times when he finally stumbled home.

I walked out quickly. Past the regulars who didn't look up. Through the door that stuck. Into the parking lot where gravel crunched under my feet.

The night air was cold and clean. It washed off the bar smell, but not the taste of wine still on my lips. Not the burn where it had touched my tongue.

The first crack in the armor I'd spent my whole life building.

I sat in my car for a long time in Murphy's lot. Engine off. Just breathing.

This was the lot where Dad had passed out in his truck. Where Mom had dragged him out crying. Where our whole family had fractured one drink at a time.

I thought about wine glasses and promises and the thin line between being strong and being selfish.

Leo was still dead. His blood money still sat in my account.

The worst part wasn't that I almost broke my promise, but that I wanted to.

What scared me most was understanding, for the first time, why Dad had chosen this place over us. Because for just a second, with that wine on my lips, the pain felt bearable.

And that terrified me more than anything.

I started the car and drove away from Murphy's. But I could still see the sign in my rearview mirror, glowing in the dark like a beacon calling me home.

Chapter Four

Understanding the Enemy

I SHOULD HAVE KNOWN the funeral would be a disaster when I caught myself planning it like a McKinsey project.

Linda was no help. She'd been in the same kitchen chair for three days, staring at nothing, making those drowning noises whenever anyone said Leo's name.

So, it fell to me to handle the logistics of burying my brother. Which felt fitting. I'd handled the logistics of his death too.

I made lists. Called funeral homes. Compared prices as if I were buying paper clips instead of a box to put my nineteen-year-old brother in.

Millfield Funeral Home wanted $8,500 for the basic package. More than the debt that got Leo killed.

I could pay for his death easier than I'd ever paid for his life. The irony tasted metallic in my mouth.

"We'll take the oak casket," I told Mr. Henderson, the funeral director. His hands smelled faintly of formaldehyde and sympathy.

"An excellent choice. Your brother will look very peaceful." Peaceful.

Leo had never been peaceful a day in his life. Even as a kid, he was all motion and noise and jokes so bad they made me laugh anyway.

Peace was the opposite of everything he'd ever been. But dead people don't get to choose how they're remembered.

The viewing was April 21st, three days after Leo died calling my name.

Uncle Mike paid for Leo to be dressed in a navy suit. It made him look like he was headed to a job interview in heaven.

The funeral home smelled of flowers trying to smother death. Heavy air freshener that burned my eyes. Organ music droned softly and slowly, hymns meant to make grief sound holy instead of empty.

Leo looked smaller in the casket. Younger. Like dying had peeled away the fear drugs had etched into his face.

People I hadn't seen in years came to stare at my dead brother. Teachers from before he dropped out. Kids from elementary school. The checkout girl from Morrison's Grocery who always asked about "that sweet Parker boy."

They told stories I'd never heard.

Leo making his class laugh with impressions of their history teacher. Leo helping Mrs. Garcia next door with groceries when she broke her hip. Leo drawing cartoons for the kindergartners at church, making them giggle with bad knock-knock jokes.

"He was so proud of you," Jessica said, a girl from Leo's grade. "He talked about you all the time. Said his sister was going to be rich and important, everything he'd never be."

Each story felt like a blade turning. They were talking about the Leo who existed before I decided my perfect reputation was worth more than his survival.

The church was packed. Every pew was full, with people standing along the back wall.

More people than I'd expected. More than Leo probably would have believed.

His whole senior class came, even though he'd dropped out years earlier. Teachers from his elementary school. Neighbors who used to hire him to mow their lawns.

The air was thick with perfume and cologne, flowers every-where. Roses, lilies, and carnations trying to choke out the smell of grief.

I sat in the front pew with the eulogy folded in my pocket. Five pages I'd written the night before, careful words about Leo's "struggles" and "challenges." Safe phrases like "he's at peace now" and "gone too soon."

All lies.

When the pastor called my name, my legs turned to water. I stood anyway and walked to the podium on feet that didn't feel like mine. The microphone was cold against my hands. I gripped it to keep from shaking.

I looked out at all the faces, hundreds of eyes waiting for me to say something that would make sense of a nine-teen-year-old shot behind a warehouse.

Something comforting.

I pulled the speech from my pocket with shaking hands. The paper rattled against the microphone.

"We gather today to remember Leo Parker," I began. My voice cracked. "A young man whose life was cut short by…"

I stopped. The words on the page blurred into ink smudges. Cut short by what? Tragedy? Circumstances? Bad luck?

My hands shook harder. The paper rustled again, loud and dry.

"Leo was…" I tried. Swallowed. "He was a person who…"

Who what? Struggled? Failed? Fought? The safe words felt like sandpaper in my throat.

I looked up, all those faces staring back, patient. Linda sat in the front row, eyes swollen, hands twisted tight in her lap.

And then I couldn't do it. Couldn't stand there and lie about what killed my brother.

"Leo died because he believed I loved him," I said.

The microphone carried my voice to every corner of the church. It came out louder than I intended. A murmur rippled through the crowd. Shifting bodies. Uneasy glances.

I crumpled the speech in my fist.

"He died with my phone number in his pocket because he thought his big sister would save him."

My voice was growing stronger now, or maybe just more desperate.

"But I chose my thesis over his life. I chose…"

The next words jammed in my throat like broken glass.

"I chose my perfect reputation over…"

I couldn't finish. Couldn't say "his survival" out loud.

Linda gasped. The sound cut through the silence like a blade. Uncle Mike started to rise from his seat. I noticed him move in the corner of my eye.

But the dam had broken. Three weeks of guilt, rage, and unbearable truth came spilling out.

"I killed my brother," I said.

The church went still. No coughing. No whispering. Even the babies stopped fussing. Hundreds of eyes locked on me. Shock. Confusion. Horror.

"I killed him with judgment," my voice shook, rising. "I killed him by deciding some people are worth saving and others aren't."

The microphone squealed, sharp and painful.

"He called me fourteen times in six weeks. Fourteen times my brother begged me to save his life. And I sent him to voicemail because I had more important things to do."

Faces stared at me as if I'd lost my mind right there in front of them. Maybe I had.

"He texted me the night he died." My hands gripped the podium until my knuckles turned white. "He said, 'I love you, sis.' And I deleted it without reading it because I had a thesis to defend."

I started crying then. Not quiet tears. The ugly kind that shakes your whole body, leaving snot running down your chin. I didn't wipe it away.

"I'm sorry, Leo." The words came out jagged. "I'm sorry I wasn't the sister you deserved. I'm sorry I let you die alone."

Uncle Mike was walking up the aisle. His footsteps echoed in the silent church. But I wasn't done.

"Don't make the same mistake I made," I said, looking out at all the faces. Teachers. Classmates. Neighbors. All their eyes were filled with pity and horror and the awkwardness of watching someone come apart. "Don't choose your comfort over someone else's life."

The congregation shifted again. Uncomfortable. Staring at the floor.

"My brother died believing love was coming to save him." My voice fell to a whisper, but the microphone caught it. "And I taught him that love has conditions."

Uncle Mike reached the podium. His hand touched my arm. Gentle but steady.

"I taught him wrong," I whispered into the microphone.

The words bounced off the stained glass windows and filled the whole church.

Uncle Mike's hand closed around my arm. Not rough, just steady. Guiding me away from the microphone like a child.

I let him lead me back to the front pew. My legs trembled so badly I almost fell.

Linda was crying so hard her whole body shook. She reached for my hand. Squeezed until it hurt. I didn't pull away.

The reception was at Linda's house. Casseroles and cold cuts covered every surface. People packed into the living room, the kitchen, spilling onto the porch. But nobody talked to me.

They talked around me. Past me. Over me.

Mrs. Perez from next door brought potato salad and set it on the counter without making eye contact. Just placed it down and walked away like I was furniture.

Leo's old English teacher, Mr. Walsh, started toward me with his hand out. Then stopped. Turned to Linda instead. "I'm so sorry for your loss." As if I wasn't standing right there.

The whispers started around 3 PM. I caught pieces.

"Can you believe—"

"In front of everyone—"

"That poor woman." Eyes flicking to Linda. Not to me.

I stood in the corner by the bookshelf, holding a paper plate with food I couldn't eat. Watching people fill the house with their sympathy for Linda, their shock about Leo, their careful silence about what I'd said.

Uncle Mike found me there an hour later.

"You should go upstairs," he said quietly. "Rest."

"I'm fine."

"Olivia." His voice dropped lower. "People are uncomfortable. It's better if you—"

"If I hide?"

His face went tired. Sad. "People don't know what to say to you."

"They could say anything. They could say, 'I'm sorry.' They could say, 'Leo mattered.' They could—"

"They're scared of you." The words came out flat. Honest. "You said something true and terrible in front of the whole town. And now they don't know how to be around you."

I looked out at the living room. All those people. All that careful distance.

"Good," I said. "They should be scared. They should feel uncomfortable."

Uncle Mike's hand touched my shoulder. "Go upstairs. Please."

I went. Through the crowded living room. Past all the people who suddenly found the walls very interesting. Up the stairs to my old bedroom.

Behind me, the conversations started up again, louder now that I was gone, like they'd been holding their breath.

Three weeks after the funeral, I made a decision that would erase everything I'd spent twenty-one years building.

I was going to kill myself on Leo's birthday: June 15th, his twentieth birthday, the one he'd never see. But first, I needed to understand something.

I needed to know what had been strong enough to kill both my father and my brother.

The pain in my chest was unbearable, like broken glass grinding under my ribs every time I breathed. Every time I thought about Leo calling my name while a gun pressed against his head.

What made alcohol worth dying for? What made drugs feel better than living?

All my life, I'd treated addiction like the enemy. Some evil that invades good people and turns them into monsters. But what if I was wrong?

What if addiction wasn't the enemy at all, but medicine for pain too big for a body to hold?

The noise in my head wouldn't stop, a loop of that final voicemail I'd never listened to. Leo saying my name over and over while I slept safely in my dorm bed, annoyed by his calls.

I needed it to stop. I needed to understand what Dad and Leo had found in their poison. What felt worth more than the people who loved them.

Maybe then I could forgive myself long enough to die.

The Millfield Liquor Store sat wedged between a Chinese takeout place and a check-cashing shop for people without bank accounts.

The same store where Dad used to buy the whiskey that killed him one swallow at a time.

The clerk behind the counter looked like he'd been selling misery since Prohibition: gray hair, yellow teeth, eyes that had watched too many people hand their lives over for bottles.

"Can I help you?" he asked, but his tone implied he already knew this was a mistake.

I walked to the whiskey aisle like it was an altar. Rows of bottles stood lined up like golden soldiers.

Jack Daniel's.

The brand that killed Dad. The brand that clung to his breath the night he lay throwing up on the bathroom floor while I was six years old and praying to be different.

"You sure about this, honey?" the clerk asked as I set the bottle on the counter. "Your daddy used to buy this same brand. Didn't end well for him."

He remembered. Of course he did. Small towns remember their tragedies. They collect them like baseball cards, swapping stories about who drank themselves into the grave and whose kids never made it out.

"I'm nothing like my father," I said.

The biggest lie I'd told since promising Leo I'd always protect him.

"That's what they all say." The clerk rang it up without looking at me. "Twenty-three fifty."

Twenty-three dollars and fifty cents. The price of betraying every promise I'd ever made to myself.

I drove to the house on Maple Street. The house where Leo built blanket forts, drew stick-figure families, and believed his big sister would always keep him safe.

Linda was at her sister's. She couldn't bear to sit inside the place where she'd raised two kids only to bury both.

I walked through the empty rooms. My footsteps echoed too loudly. The April air seeped through cracked windows, damp and cold, carrying the smell of wet dirt and something rotting in the yard.

In Dad's room, I pulled open his nightstand drawer. The wood groaned. Inside was a small cedar box with tarnished brass hinges. Cool and smooth in my hands. Lighter than I remembered.

I lifted the lid. Inside, on faded velvet, lay Grandpa's compass.

My breath caught. Dad had given it to me when I was eight, the brass still warm from his hands. I'd kept it by my bed for years, gripping it every night like it could protect me. But when I left for college, I put it back because I knew then it hadn't saved him.

Now I picked it up. The brass was cold, heavy as stone. The glass face was cracked, a thin fracture splitting north from south. Like something inside it had broken trying to point the way.

I sat on Dad's bed. The mattress sagged into the valley worn by his body. The sheets smelled like Old Spice, cigarettes, and something sour underneath.

And suddenly I was eight again. Small and hopeful, sitting beside him. His hand on my shoulder. His eyes clear for once.

"I'm giving it to you because you're my compass, Olivia. You always know what's right."

His voice had been gentle. Full of hope.

"Promise me you'll never lose that."

"I promise, Daddy."

The words slipped out of me again now, a whisper in an empty room. But I hadn't just lost my compass. I'd followed it straight off a cliff.

I closed my fingers around the brass. The cracked glass bit into my palm. My throat tightened. Tears blurred the compass until it swam in my hand. I shoved it in my pocket and went downstairs. Each step heavy, dragging.

The house was a museum of what was gone.

Dad's chair still reeked of cigarettes and regret. Leo's room was still plastered with band posters from before the drugs made music sound like static.

I dropped into Dad's chair. The whiskey bottle weighed down my lap.

On the side table, a photo of seven-year-old Leo. Building a fort, tongue poking out in concentration, eyes lit up with trust.

The compass burned against my thigh like a hot coal.

"Here's to understanding," I said to the empty room. My voice cracked. "Here's to finding out why you chose this over us."

I twisted the cap. Metal against metal. The smell burst out sharp and chemical, burning the back of my throat.

For my entire life, I'd built my whole identity on one promise. I will never, ever, EVER be like my father.

Every late night at the library. Every scholarship. Every water glass at parties while everyone else drank beer. That promise had carried me. Protected me.

I set Dad's compass on the table. Raised the bottle.

The first sip hit like fire. Not warmth. Flames. Like drinking gasoline. My throat seized. Tears sprang to my eyes.

It tasted like betrayal. Like rust. Like rotting fruit. But beneath it, something shifted.

The noise stopped.

For the first time since 8:17 a.m., since Detective Doyle's voice shattered my world, my head went quiet. The loop of Leo calling my name was gone. The endless guilt reel was gone.

Just... silence.

"Oh my God." The words came out in a sob. My hands shook so hard that the bottle rattled against my teeth. "This is what you found."

Not the alcohol. The quiet. The blessed, beautiful silence.

I drank again. It burned even worse. But I didn't care.

Every swallow was a betrayal and relief wrestling inside me. My limbs tingled. My fingers went numb. But the quiet spread deeper.

For the first time in weeks, I could breathe without choking. I could exist without feeling like the weight of Leo's death was crushing me.

The room softened. Angles blurred. Dad's chair felt less like bones and more like cotton.

The compass needle wavered. My vision blurred.

I kept drinking. The bottle grew lighter. My head grew heavy. The room tilted like a boat rocking on water.

My entire life of sobriety dissolved like sugar in the rain. I had become just like my father. Just like Leo. Just like everyone I'd judged as too weak.

And for the first time since Leo died, that felt like the only place I belonged.

Chapter Five

The Medicine I Needed

THE FIRST NIGHT I slept without nightmares changed everything.

For three weeks since Leo died, sleep had been a battlefield. Every time I shut my eyes, his face was there. The hollow eyes from his last texts, eyes that trusted me to save him. Every dream ended with a gunshot and Detective Doyle's voice saying, "He died believing you'd save him."

But after half a bottle of Jack Daniel's, I slept. Eight straight hours in Dad's old chair. No blood on concrete. No replay of the end.

I woke with sunlight spilling through windows that hadn't been opened since Dad died. For ten sweet seconds, I forgot. Forgot Leo was gone. Forgot the bloodstain behind the warehouse. Forgot the silence of a phone that would never buzz again.

Then it all crashed back. The empty bottle on the floor, the taste of betrayal still on my tongue, the familiar weight pressing down on my chest. But I'd slept. Actually slept. For the first time in weeks.

The bottle sat on the table like a prescription I'd written for myself. Medicine for pain too big for a body to hold.

I told myself it was research. Fieldwork. A temporary study with a planned end date. I wasn't becoming Dad. I was just trying to understand what killed him and Leo before I joined them in June.

But even as I thought it, my hand was already reaching for the bottle. Checking if there was any medicine left.

The second night, I wasn't alone.

I was sipping the same glass for hours, trying to make it last, when I heard movement in the next room. Not voices. Just the soft rustle of people who'd forgotten how to be loud. I crept to the doorway.

Dad sat in his chair, but younger. The age when he still read me bedtime stories. Leo sat cross-legged on the floor, stacking invisible blocks. His hands worked carefully, as if he was building something important.

They didn't look at me.

Dad held a compass in his palm. The brass one he'd given me. Only this one wasn't cracked. The needle spun, searching.

"It's hard to find your way," Dad said softly, eyes on the compass. "When you're lost."

Leo added another block to his fort. "Some paths look the same," he said. "But they don't lead to the same place."

Dad's compass kept spinning. Never settling.

"I chose the bottle," Dad said. "Every time there was a choice, I chose the bottle."

"I chose the needle," Leo said. His hands didn't stop moving. "Every time I was scared, I chose the needle."

I stepped into the room. They both looked up. Their eyes weren't angry. Not sad either. Just... knowing.

"What will you choose?" Leo asked.

Dad held out the compass. The needle still spun.

"The bottle makes it stop," Dad said. "For a while."

"But it doesn't change direction," Leo added. "It just makes you forget you're walking in circles."

I reached for the compass. My hand passed through it like smoke.

"I don't know where to go," I whispered.

Leo smiled. That same smile from when he was eight and believed I could fix anything.

"You will," he said. "When you're ready to stop running."

Dad walked to the window. Snow fell outside, though it was May.

"Winter's coming," he said. "Long winter."

"But spring always follows," Leo said, placing the last block on his fort. "If you survive the cold."

They started to fade.

"Wait," I called. "I don't understand."

Leo's fort collapsed. He didn't look sad. He just smiled and began rebuilding.

"You will," he said. "When you need to."

Dad's compass hit the floor with a soft thud. It cracked again, the needle pointing nowhere. But for a moment, I could feel where north was. And I knew I wasn't ready to follow it.

Two weeks after I broke my sobriety, Linda came home.

She'd been staying at her sister's, trying to stitch herself back together after burying her son. I hadn't expected her so soon. I hadn't had time to hide the evidence of my "research."

She found me at three in the afternoon on a Tuesday, passed out in Dad's chair. An empty whiskey bottle lay on the floor. Leo's childhood photos were scattered across my lap like they'd spilled out of me in my sleep.

"Olivia."

Her voice cut through the fog like a knife. I opened my eyes. She stood in the doorway still wearing the black funeral dress. The one she hadn't taken off in two weeks. She looked smaller somehow, like grief had shrunk her body.

"What time is it?" I mumbled.

"Three o'clock. In the afternoon." Her voice was steady, but beneath it, I could hear something breaking.

I tried to sit up straighter, to make myself look like anything but what I was: a drunk in my father's chair, drowning in failure.

"I was just... looking at old pictures of Leo. Must've dozed off."

Linda walked in, picked up the empty bottle, and held it to the light like it was evidence in a case she already knew the ending to.

"How long?" she asked.

"How long what?"

"How long have you been drinking?"

The words hung between us like an accusation. I could lie. Say this was the first time. Say I just needed help sleeping after the funeral.

But her eyes already knew.

"Two weeks," I whispered.

Her eyes closed as if I'd struck her. When she opened them, they brimmed with tears.

"Just like your father," she said. No anger. Just devastation. "Sitting in his chair, drinking his poison, making excuses."

"It's not the same."

"How is it different?"

"I'm not hurting anyone but myself. I'm not screaming or throwing things or breaking promises."

"You think watching someone you love destroy themselves doesn't hurt?" Linda's voice cracked. "You think waiting for a call that says you've joined your father and brother doesn't count as pain?"

Then she broke. Not the quiet tears she'd shed since Leo died, but deep, raw sobs that ripped from her chest.

"I can't do this again," she cried. "I can't bury another child."

The words hit me like bullets. Another child. She was already grieving me as if I were gone.

"I'm not going to die," I said. But the lie tasted bitter because I remembered my plan for Leo's birthday.

"Yes, you are," she sobbed. "You're going to die like your father. Alone. Sick. Convinced we were better off without you."

She collapsed into Dad's chair, folding in on herself as if strings had been cut. Her shoulders shook with sobs that sounded like dying.

"Please," she whispered. "Please don't make me lose you too. Please don't make me bury all my children."

Something cracked inside me watching her. This woman who had held the family together through Dad's worst years, who absorbed his rage so Leo and I didn't have to, who only ever asked that we make it out alive. And here I was, destroying myself in the same chair, forcing her to relive it all.

I dropped to my knees beside her and pulled her close. Her lavender shampoo mixed with the salt of her tears.

"I'm sorry," I sobbed into her shoulder. "I'm so sorry, Mom."

We clung to each other like we were drowning. And maybe we were. Drowning in grief, guilt, and the truth that addiction doesn't just kill the person who drinks; it kills everyone who loves them, one betrayal at a time.

"I was going to kill myself on Leo's birthday," I blurted. "I was going to join him so you wouldn't have to worry anymore."

Linda pulled back, grabbed my face in both hands, and forced me to meet her eyes.

"Don't you dare," she said, fierce and sharp. "Don't you dare take away the only child I have left. Don't you dare make Leo's death meaningless by throwing away the life he died believing was worth saving."

"I don't know how to live with what I did."

"Then learn," she said. "Get help. Fight this disease. But don't you dare give up on the daughter I raised to be stronger than her pain."

She was right. Leo had died believing I was strong enough to save him. The least I could do was try to save myself.

"The McKinsey job starts in six weeks," she said, wiping my face with her sleeve. "Six weeks to decide if you're going to be the daughter who survived this family or another casualty."

"I don't know if I can do it alone."

"Then don't," she said. "Get help. Go to meetings. See a therapist. But don't sit here drinking yourself to death in your father's chair."

I wanted to promise I'd stop. I wanted to say this moment would change everything. But promises from someone who had already broken the most important one meant nothing.

So I said, "I'll try."

"Trying isn't enough," she said. "Your father tried for fifteen years. Leo tried. Trying without help is just giving up more slowly."

She was right. But admitting I needed help meant admitting I wasn't different. It meant facing that the golden girl was gone. That I had inherited the family disease along with the blue eyes and the stubborn jaw.

"I'm scared," I whispered.

"Good," Linda said, pulling me close again. "Scared means you're still alive. Scared means there's something left worth fighting for."

That night, I poured the rest of the whiskey down the kitchen sink. I went to bed sober for the first time in two weeks.

The nightmares came back. Leo's voice whispering, *I love you, sis.* The sound of dirt hitting his coffin. Detective Doyle saying, *He died believing you'd save him.*

But I stayed sober through them because Linda was asleep down the hall, and I couldn't bear the thought of her waking up to find another empty bottle. Another broken promise.

It was the first battle in a war I didn't believe I could win, but it was a start.

Going back to Columbus for graduation felt like slipping into a costume, pretending to be someone I'd already buried.

I was five days sober, five nightmare-filled, crawling-out-of-my-skin days. Every hour stretched like a year. My body begged for relief, but Linda rode shotgun, and her presence felt like a leash I couldn't break.

My dorm room looked untouched, as if time had frozen the morning Leo died. The McKinsey offer letter still sat on my desk, a promise of a future that felt impossible and terrifying at the same time. Six weeks until Chicago. Six weeks until I had to look like someone who had her life together.

The graduation ceremony was torture. Sitting in that folding chair while families cheered, all I could think about was

Leo missing mine. How proud he'd been of me getting the McKinsey offer. How he'd told everyone his sister was going to be rich and important and everything he'd never be.

When they called my name for summa cum laude, the applause felt hollow, like clapping for a mask, not a person.

Professor Williams found me afterward, his face lit up with pride I didn't deserve.

"Olivia! Congratulations. McKinsey is lucky to have you."

Lucky. They were getting a girl who let her brother die for eight thousand dollars. A girl who nearly drank herself to death in her father's chair. But Williams didn't know about the whiskey or the nightmares or the night Linda caught me sinking.

He saw the golden girl everyone thought I was, the girl who had never existed.

"Thank you," I said because it was easier than explaining that success felt meaningless when it cost me everything that mattered.

That night, Linda and I shared a hotel room near campus. Two beds. One unspoken understanding that I wasn't ready to be alone with my thoughts yet.

"I'm proud of you," she said while we brushed our teeth.

"For graduating?"

"For staying sober today. For fighting instead of surrendering."

Five days sober. Not much. But something. A shaky foundation I wasn't sure would hold.

Apartment hunting in Chicago was my first real test.

The agent was a polished woman in her forties. She showed me three places in Lincoln Park, each one shinier and more expensive than the last. The kind of apartments where people lived perfect, successful lives.

"This one has a wine refrigerator," she said, sliding open a sleek cabinet. "Perfect for entertaining."

A wine refrigerator. Of course.

"I don't drink," I said. Technically true, for the past week.

"Oh! Then sparkling water, maybe."

The apartment gleamed. Clean lines. Tall windows. A space built for pretending you were someone else.

"I'll take it," I said.

"Don't you want to think about it?"

What I wanted was to get out before that refrigerator started whispering to me. What I wanted was a place far enough from Millfield that nobody knew what I used to be. A place to learn how to be sober in a world that felt unbearable without a buffer.

The McKinsey bonus covered the deposit and three months' rent. Clean money buying me a shot at staying clean.

The week before I left, I packed up my childhood, trying to figure out how to carry a life that didn't include bottles.

Linda folded clothes beside me, wrapping frames in newspaper, careful around the places where I used to hide evidence. We didn't talk about the whiskey I'd poured down the sink or the empties I'd tossed in the trash. We just packed what was worth keeping and left the rest behind.

"You don't have to do this alone," she said on my last night in Millfield. We sat in the same living room where I'd broken my sobriety. It looked like just a room now, not a crime scene.

"I know."

"There are meetings in Chicago. Therapists. People who've fought and won."

"I know."

"And there's me. Always me. No matter how far away you go, there's me."

I looked at her. Really looked. I saw strength deeper than survival and love stronger than disappointment.

"I love you, Mom."

"I love you too, sweetheart. More than you'll ever know."

The next morning, I loaded my car with boxes and bags, along with the fragile hope of staying sober long enough to deserve what lay ahead.

Linda hugged me like she was letting go of something precious. Maybe she was.

"Call me when you get there."

"I will."

I drove toward Chicago with empty hands and a head full of hope, telling myself that moving away could be enough if I was brave enough to make it true.

The golden girl who never drank was gone. In her place was someone who carried her father's disease but chose to fight it.

McKinsey was getting the right Parker after all, the one who knew what it meant to lose everything and still start over. The one who'd learned that the hardest, most important job she'd ever have was staying sober.

Chapter Six

Wine Is Different

THE WINE BAR ON Rush Street smelled like money and possibility.

Two years after Leo died, I still woke at 3 a.m. every night, his voice echoing in my head. My chest felt hollowed out, like someone had scooped out everything vital and left me caved in.

I'd tried everything: meditation apps that made me want to throw my phone, exercise that left me shaking and sick, and sleeping pills that brought nightmares worse than being awake.

Nothing worked. But in that wine bar, watching Chicago's polished professionals swirl glasses of Burgundy and Sauvignon Blanc, something shifted.

These weren't broken people drowning their sorrows. These were consultants, lawyers, executives. They used wine as a bridge, crossing from the sharp edges of work into something softer. A way to relax without falling apart.

At client dinners, I'd seen wine do more than food or numbers ever could. Colleagues leaning in, discussing vintages and regions like old friends. Deals closed over a shared bottle.

"The Piedmont region produces some of the most complex Barolos," one managing director told a client. "The 2009 vintage was exceptional."

By dessert, the contract was signed. Even Linda's sister Carol had a glass of Chardonnay with dinner every night. She wasn't an alcoholic; she was a normal adult with a normal glass of wine.

Maybe I'd been wrong all along. Maybe my childhood promise had been an overreaction. Maybe there was a world of difference between Dad's whiskey-soaked destruction and the cultured, civilized wine culture of Chicago.

The wine shop near my apartment was nothing like the liquor store Dad used to haunt. Soft lighting, shelves labeled by region and varietal, and staff who spoke about bottles the way other people spoke about books.

"Something light," I told the woman behind the counter. "For evenings. To unwind."

She handed me a Pinot Grigio from Oregon. "Crisp. Clean. Perfect for after work."

That night, I poured a small glass and sat at my window facing Lake Michigan.

It didn't taste like the poison Dad drank. No fire. No gasoline. Just smooth and faintly sweet, with gentle warmth spreading through my chest instead of burning it raw.

More importantly, it worked.

For the first time since Leo's death, the constant replay stopped. The guilt loosened its grip just enough for me to breathe. The pain was still there, but quieter. Manageable.

I slept eight hours without a single nightmare.

Within a month, wine had become routine. One glass at night. Not to get drunk. I told myself that over and over. Just enough to turn down the volume. Just enough to rest.

At work, the difference showed. I wasn't exhausted all the time. I could focus in meetings. I stopped flinching every time my phone buzzed. The tight coil that had kept me hyper-alert through college finally began to unwind.

"You seem more settled," my manager, Jennifer, said after a client presentation. "Chicago suits you."

She was right. Wine was suiting me. Wine was giving me back the ability to live.

Success came quickly after that.

My salary was more money than my family had ever seen. For the first time, I wasn't worried about rent or groceries. Better still, I could help Linda.

It started small. Five hundred dollars for an "early birthday gift." Then a thousand for house repairs. Then regular monthly checks I called "loans" but knew she'd never pay back.

Within six months, she cut back to part-time. No more double shifts at the diner. No more limping home with sore feet.

"I don't know how to thank you," she said one night over the phone.

"Just be happy, Mom. You've earned it."

Every glass felt justified. Every sip a way of becoming the daughter who solved problems instead of creating them.

Wine wasn't indulgence. Wine was self-care. Wine was strategy.

So the boundaries shifted. One glass became two. Then three. Weekends got their own rules. Why only feel calm Monday through Friday? If wine helped me at work, surely it could help me in life.

A glass at Saturday lunch. Wine with groceries on Sunday. A toast whenever there was something worth celebrating, and gradually, everything was worth celebrating.

And I was functioning better than ever. Sharper in meetings. More articulate with clients. More social with colleagues. Wine didn't weaken me. It polished me.

"You should join us for wine tasting," my colleague Sarah said after a dinner with German automotive executives. I'd navigated the wine list like a pro, and they'd been impressed.

"You clearly have a palate," she smiled.

The Chicago Wine Society met once a month in different restaurants. Young professionals, learning about varietals and terroir, sipping while listening to sommeliers describe soil and climate as if they were poetry.

"Wine is about terroir," one explained at my first tasting. "Soil, climate, tradition. All combining into flavor."

I loved that idea. Wine as geography. As history. As art. It made drinking feel intellectual. Elevated.

That's where I met Raymond.

He sat across from me at a Burgundy tasting, studying his glass like it held secrets. Dark hair, steady eyes, a confidence that wasn't loud but grounded.

"What do you think of this one?" he asked, holding up a deep red.

"Earthier than I expected," I said, proud of how confident my voice sounded. "Something mineral about it."

"Exactly." He smiled. "That's the limestone in the soil. That's what makes Burgundy distinctive."

He was a photographer, sharing stories about family vineyards in Europe. Stories about tradition and patience. He made wine feel like culture, like adventure, like sophistication wrapped in a glass.

Over three tastings, our conversation stretched and deepened. Then he said something that fit perfectly with what I was already telling myself.

"Wine is civilized drinking. It's about appreciation, not intoxication. About understanding the story each bottle tells."

And I believed him.

Raymond and I started meeting for dinners at restaurants chosen for their wine lists. He'd research unusual varietals and regions. I'd spend hours online studying vocabulary so I could keep up.

My daily consumption grew, but it felt justified. Professional development.

"Olivia's our secret weapon for entertaining," Jennifer said after I navigated a German client's complex wine list. "You make McKinsey look sophisticated."

At a happy hour, I overheard two partners whispering about a wealthy prospect.

"We'll need someone who can hold their own in a high-end restaurant.""What about Olivia? She knows more than half the sommeliers."

They assigned me to the account. A two-million-dollar contract partly secured because I could pronounce *Gewürztraminer* and recommend the right Loire Valley vintage.

The message was clear: wine knowledge was power.

Raymond made wine feel like a doorway into sophistication I never thought I'd walk through.

Six months into dating, he took me to a fancy restaurant for my birthday. The sommelier recognized him right away.

"Raymond, good to see you. Pairing tonight?"

"Actually," Raymond said, smiling at me. "I'd like my girlfriend to choose. She has excellent taste."

My heart raced, but I'd already studied the list. "The Sancerre, 2016 Henri Bourgeois. And for the main course, the Barolo, 2012 Giacomo Conterno."

"Exceptional," the sommelier said. "One of our prized bottles."

When he left, Raymond reached across the table. "That was incredible."

"Too much?" I asked, worried about the cost.

"Perfect," he said. "You have instincts that can't be taught."

But it wasn't just instincts. I'd been studying obsessively. Wine was my hobby, my career edge, my daily ritual. Two glasses with dinner became three. Then four. Weekend tastings blurred into weekend drinking.

The morning after that birthday dinner, I woke with a headache and a flicker of memory, stumbling as we left the restaurant.

"Did I seem drunk last night?" I asked as Raymond brewed coffee.

He paused too long. "You were lively. Animated. It was one of our best conversations with a sommelier."

Something in his voice was careful. Too careful.

"I just felt more confident than usual."

"Wine does that," he said, handing me a cup. But he didn't quite meet my eyes.

After that, his concerns sharpened.

"You've had three glasses, I've had one," he said one night over pasta.

"I drink faster," I replied, waving the server for a refill. "Besides, I'm studying this region. Research."

"Olivia." His voice was gentle but steady. "You panic when restaurants don't serve wine. You keep bottles in your office. You can't sleep without drinking first."

Each point landed like a stone. True. But also reasonable. Wine helped me sleep. Wine helped me work. Wine kept me from falling apart.

"This is nothing like my father's drinking," I snapped.

Raymond's face shifted. "How do you know what his drinking was like?"

"Because he drank whiskey to get drunk and violent. I drink wine to be sophisticated. To function. It's not the same."

Something flickered across his face. Recognition. Maybe fear.

"I know," he said quickly. "I'm not saying you have a problem. I just thought... maybe we could try activities that don't revolve around wine."

It felt like an attack. Wine wasn't just what we did. It was how I survived. How I managed grief and pressure and the constant noise in my head.

"Wine is part of who I am now," I said. "It's not something I want to give up."

Raymond looked at me, his expression unreadable. Sadness, maybe. Or disappointment.

He didn't push. Not that night. But I noticed the shift. How he left earlier when I opened a second bottle. How he suggested coffee instead of tastings. How he went from encouraging my education to watching me with quiet dread.

I told myself he was overreacting. That he didn't understand the difference between sophisticated wine culture and the kind of desperate drinking that had gutted my family. But deep down, I wondered if he saw something I couldn't yet.

Something that was already beginning to undo us.

Wine had saved me, given me success, sleep, a way to bear Leo's absence.

I didn't yet see that the same thing saving me was also the thing destroying everything else I loved, including the man who'd first held the door open to the world that was slowly pulling me under.

By our first anniversary, Raymond started asking questions I didn't want to answer.

We were at a new farm-to-table spot in Logan Square. Trendy, all local sourcing, the kind of place the Chicago food scene adored. I asked for the wine list, and the server looked embarrassed.

"We're still building our program," she said. "Just house red, house white, and a few local beers."

My stomach tightened. House wines were usually cheap and cloying, meant for people who couldn't tell the difference.

"What about cocktails?" Raymond asked, reading my face.

"I don't drink cocktails," I said. "Could we maybe go somewhere else?"

Surprise flickered across his face. Then something else: recognition. "The food here is supposed to be amazing. Can't you just have water for one meal?"

The suggestion felt impossible. Not because I couldn't function without alcohol, but because good food deserved good wine. "Eating without wine is like listening to music through broken speakers."

"Most people enjoy food without wine, Olivia."

The comment stung. "Most people don't understand flavor profiles. They're missing half the experience."

He leaned forward, voice low but steady. "Do you know what my father used to tell me? *'Raymond, you can't appreciate fine cuisine without the right pairing. It's uncivilized.'*"

"Your father had good taste," I said quickly.

"My father was a functioning alcoholic for twenty years." His voice was flat. "High-functioning. Attorney. Big house. Wine cellar worth more than cars."

I froze. He'd never mentioned this before.

"He never got sloppy drunk," Raymond continued. "Never missed work. Never raised his voice. Just like you. But he also couldn't eat a meal, attend an event, or relax without alcohol. Just like you."

My chest tightened. "That's completely different. I'm not—"

"He died at fifty-two. Liver failure." Raymond's voice shook. "The last thing he said to me was that wine wasn't dangerous because it was sophisticated."

The restaurant felt too warm, too bright. "Why didn't you tell me?"

"Because I wanted you to be different." His eyes were wet. "Do you know why I know so much about wine? Because I grew up watching it kill him, sip by sip."

Three weeks later, he tried a different angle.

"I need to ask you something," he said at my apartment. I was opening my second bottle of the night. "Will you go one week without drinking? Seven days. If wine is just culture and appreciation like you say, it should be easy."

My hands froze on the corkscrew. "That's not fair. You know I use wine to manage the stress of Leo's death."

"My father used it for work stress. Same excuse."

"This is different."

"How?" He stepped closer. "How is it different? Because you cry about your brother while you drink instead of staying silent like he did?"

The accusation hit like a slap.

"You bastard. You don't get to use Leo against me."

"I'm not using him against you," Raymond said, his voice trembling. "I'm saying grief is just another excuse people give themselves to drink every day. You think you're the first person to lose someone and reach for a bottle? You think that makes it less dangerous?"

"Get out."

"Olivia—"

"GET OUT!" I hurled the wine bottle at the wall. It exploded, glass and Pinot Grigio spraying across the kitchen. "Get out of my apartment and don't come back."

Raymond looked at the shards, then at me. Instead of leaving, he walked to the fridge and pulled out the broom.

"What are you doing?"

"Cleaning up," he said, sweeping the glass into a pile. "Before you step on it."

"I told you to leave."

"I heard you." He kept sweeping. "But I'm not walking out until we finish this."

"There's nothing to finish. You think I'm a drunk like my father. I think you're wrong. That's it."

He stopped and looked straight at me. "When's the last time you went twenty-four hours without alcohol?"

My mouth opened, then closed. I couldn't remember. Maybe months. Maybe longer.

"When's the last time you had sex completely sober?"

That one hit harder. "That's none of your business."

"It is," he said. "I'm your boyfriend. Or I was, until you threw a bottle at the wall and told me to leave." He went back to sweeping, his motions sharp. "Do you know what my mother used to say about my father's drinking?"

"I don't care."

"She said he was the most sophisticated drunk she'd ever met. He could talk vintages while putting away a bottle and a half every night. He could function at work, charm clients, and never embarrass himself. Right up until the day his liver failed." Raymond dumped the glass into the trash.

"I'm not your father."

"No, you're not." He leaned the broom against the wall and faced me. "You're the woman I love, and I'm watching you become exactly like him. And I don't know how to stop it."

His voice cracked on that last line. For the first time that night, he sounded scared.

"Raymond—"

"I can't stand by while you kill yourself with expensive wine and call it culture," he said. "But I can't walk away either."

We stood in the kitchen, the air thick with the smell of spilled wine, both of us listening to our hearts break.

"So what do we do?" I whispered.

"I don't know. But throwing bottles and telling me to leave isn't the answer."

My eyes drifted to the wet streak on the wall where the wine was dripping down. The bottle had cost sixty dollars. I'd smashed sixty dollars of wine to prove I didn't have a drinking problem.

Even I could see the irony.

"I'm scared," I said quietly.

"Of what?"

"Of what happens if I stop." My throat tightened. "Wine is the only thing that makes Leo's death bearable. It's the only thing that makes me feel normal."

Raymond stepped closer. "What if normal isn't supposed to hurt this much? What if grief isn't supposed to need medication every single day?"

I wanted to fight him. Tell him he didn't understand. That he'd never lost anyone the way I lost Leo.

But staring at the broken glass on my floor, something inside me cracked. Something I'd been holding together with sheer will.

"I don't know how to stop," I whispered.

Raymond's face hardened. "That's what I was afraid you'd say."

He grabbed paper towels and started scrubbing the wall, not gently, as if he were cleaning up after a child who'd made a mess.

"Raymond—"

"Don't." His voice was flat, dead. "Just don't."

He stayed that night, but on the couch. He said it was so I wouldn't cut myself on glass. But I knew it was because he couldn't stand to lie next to me.

I lay awake in bed, listening to him toss and turn in the living room, both of us pretending to sleep while the smell of spilled wine hung in the air.

In the morning, he made coffee in silence and set a cup down for me without looking.

"Thank you," I said.

He nodded once. Distant. Polite. Like I was a client, not the woman he'd once told he loved.

"I have a shoot today," he said, scrolling his phone. "I'll be back late."

"Okay."

But nothing about us was okay anymore. His eyes saw someone he didn't recognize. Someone who had disappointed him beyond repair.

He left without kissing me goodbye.

By ten a.m., I'd opened a bottle of Chardonnay. I told myself it was to calm the shaking in my hands, not because I needed it. But it tasted like shame. Like broken promises. Like the slow death of everything I'd built in Chicago.

And the worst part was it still worked. For a few hours, it numbed the pain, even as it pushed Raymond further away and every sip proved him right.

Chapter Seven

Shattered Crystal, Shattered Life

THE PENINSULA HOTEL BALLROOM smelled of money and ambition. Crystal chandeliers glittered overhead, casting soft light across marble floors. The air buzzed with polished laughter, the kind that floated above champagne glasses and whispered deals. Three hundred of Chicago's most powerful people gathered in one room, each one calculating and charming, each one waiting for the right moment to turn small talk into million-dollar contracts.

But before that, I was still in my apartment bathroom. The bright light above the mirror made my face look pale and tight. I leaned close, holding the lipstick with fingers that wouldn't stop shaking. I pressed hard to steady it, but my hand trembled anyway.

Jennifer's voice kept looping in my head.

"Land Carrington tonight and you're golden. Miss it and you'll be waiting another year."

The Carrington account. Two million dollars in consulting fees. The kind of client that would elevate me to senior associate, the kind of win that told everyone else in the firm I was worth watching.

But the thought of stepping into that ballroom made my chest tighten. What if I said the wrong thing? What if I didn't belong? What if they looked at me and saw through the dress and makeup, saw that I was still just a girl from Millfield pretending to be sophisticated?

I couldn't walk in like that. I needed something to quiet it all.

The first glass of wine went down at six, cold and sharp in my throat as I zipped up my dress. My heart slowed a little. My breath evened out. The second glass came while I dragged eyeliner across my eyelid, and this time my hand was steady. The line came out smooth.

But then the mirror turned cruel. Just for a second, Leo's face looked back at me instead of my own. Hollow. Desperate. The same eyes from his final text. The ones that had believed I would save him. I poured a third glass.

The fourth came while I fussed with my hair one last time. My hands had stopped shaking, replaced by that familiar warm buzz spreading behind my eyes. The world softened around the edges. The panic melted, replaced by a false glow of confidence.

When I stepped out of the bathroom, Raymond was on the couch. He hadn't slept in my bed all week. Still in his work clothes, his tie loose, and his phone glowing in his hand. He didn't look up right away.

"Maybe go easy tonight?" he said finally, his eyes still fixed on the screen. "This is important for your career."

His voice felt like an accusation. Like he thought I didn't know what I was doing. Like he thought I couldn't handle myself.

"I know exactly how much I can drink," I snapped, sharper than I intended. "This isn't college. It's networking."

He looked at me then, that flat, empty expression that had been on his face since our fight.

"Right," he said. "Sophisticated."

"I meant what I said. I'm fine."

He gave one small nod, polite but cold. "Have a good time."

No kiss. No good luck. Just that hollow distance that comes when someone has already let go but hasn't figured out how to walk away.

Crystal light everywhere. That's what I remember most. The chandeliers threw sparkles across the marble as if we were standing inside a jewelry box. Servers glided past with champagne flutes balanced on trays. Three hundred voices hummed together. Rich, confident, plotting their next million-dollar move.

I found Jennifer at the bar. Her face was already pink. Third glass, maybe fourth.

"Olivia!" She waved me over, her smile stretching wide. "Come here. I want you to meet David Carrington."

My heart jumped. This was it. The account worth two million dollars. The promotion I'd been chasing for a year.

David Carrington looked exactly like his company bio: late fifties, silver hair swept back, and a handshake that felt like closing a deal. His eyes crinkled when he smiled.

"Jennifer's been singing your praises," he said.

"I hope I can live up to them." I took the wine glass a server offered, having lost count somewhere around five. Maybe six.

"And this," David said, turning slightly, "is my wife, Margaret."

Everything stopped.

Margaret Carrington stood there in silver silk. Perfect hair. Perfect posture. Perfect everything. The CEO who'd built an empire from nothing, the woman whose Fortune magazine interview I'd kept taped above my desk through four years of college.

My hero.

"Ms. Carrington." The words tumbled out, breathless and too eager. "It's such an honor to meet you."

I stuck out my hand, holding it there like a kid meeting someone famous. Her handshake was brief. Cold. Like touching refrigerated meat.

"Thank you," she said, flat and bored.

But I couldn't help myself. The wine loosened something inside me. Eight years of admiration came pouring out.

"I've followed your career since I was sixteen," I said, the words coming fast, stumbling over each other. "That Fortune article about building Carrington Media? I cut it out and kept it in my scholarship folder. You inspired me."

Margaret's eyebrow lifted a fraction, as if I'd said something vaguely amusing.

"How lovely," she said.

Lovely. That was it.

I kept talking anyway, unable to stop myself.

"That quote you gave about refusing to let your past define your future? I read it every time I wanted to quit, when college got hard, when I thought I didn't belong. You showed me it was possible. You proved that girls from nowhere could—"

"That's very sweet," Margaret replied, her voice capable of freezing water.

Margaret paused, turning her head slightly. Not toward me, but toward a woman standing near the bar. A woman I hadn't noticed before. Expensive suit, phone in her hand. She'd been watching our conversation.

Margaret lifted one finger, a small gesture. The woman nodded, pulled out her phone, and started typing something.

Then Margaret was gone, moving through the crowd like she owned every molecule of air in the room. She just walked away while I was mid-sentence, not even glancing back.

I stood there with my hand still half-raised, mouth hanging open, and my brain struggling to understand what just happened.

The woman with the phone stayed, her eyes sweeping over me once, assessing, as if she were taking inventory. Then she turned and spoke quietly into her phone.

I felt exposed under that look. Like Margaret hadn't just dismissed me; she'd marked me, filed me away for later.

David gave me an apologetic smile. "Don't mind Margaret. She's under pressure with the quarterly earnings." But it felt personal.

The Margaret Carrington from TV was warm and inspiring. She talked about mentoring young women, about remembering where you came from, about lifting others up.

The Margaret Carrington who just walked away from me was ice. She looked at me like I was dirt on her shoe, like I wasn't worth her time. Like I was exactly what I'd spent my whole life running from: a girl from Millfield who didn't belong here.

My hands shook. I grabbed another glass from a passing tray and drank half of it in one swallow.

"You okay?" Jennifer touched my elbow.

"Fine." The lie came easily. "I'm fine." But I wasn't fine.

The woman I'd admired for eight years had just dismissed me like trash. I drank the rest of the glass and reached for another.

The first hour improved. Or at least I convinced myself it did.

I explained pricing models to David's team and made them laugh with stories about difficult clients. I timed my jokes perfectly. They leaned in close, nodding and asking questions.

"You really get our industry," David said. "Most consultants just regurgitate generic strategies."

"Every business tells a different story," I said. "Cookie-cutter solutions don't work."

The servers kept my glass full. I kept drinking, telling myself it was just nerves. Big accounts made me thirsty.

But I kept seeing Leo between conversations. A sandy-haired guy at the bar. A laugh that sounded exactly like his at seven years old. A face in the crowd that flickered. Just enough to make me think he was really there, waiting for me.

Each glimpse felt like a knife between my ribs. I washed them down with more wine.

By the second hour, heat pressed against my skin. My cheeks burned. Words spilled faster, looser. But David's group didn't seem to notice. They laughed, nodded, and asked more questions. Other executives drifted over to listen.

I was performing perfectly. Jennifer caught my eye from across the room, lifted her glass, and gave me a thumbs-up.

The promotion was mine. I could feel it. That's when I pulled out my phone.

A Facebook memory popped up on the screen. Three years ago. Leo and me at Linda's birthday dinner. He'd been thin in that photo, but his eyes were clear and bright. He was laughing at something I'd said, his arm draped over my shoulders like it would stay there forever. He looked so young, so hopeful, so alive.

The ballroom tilted sideways. I grabbed another glass from a server and gulped half.

"Everything all right?" David asked.

"Perfect." I shoved my phone back in my purse. "Just checking messages."

But Leo's face was burned into my vision now. The way he'd looked at me in that photo, like I could fix anything. Like his big sister was strong enough to save the world.

That's when the conversation changed.

"This city's falling apart," Robert Brooks said, David's CRO, already slurring from his fourth martini. "Can't walk two blocks downtown without tripping over some homeless junkie."

Junkie.

That word. The same word the neighbors whispered at Leo's funeral when they thought I couldn't hear.

My fingers squeezed the wine glass stem. I forced a professional nod. Like the insult hadn't just sliced me wide open.

"Last week—" David's face flushed red with drink. His voice got louder. "Some pathetic addict tried robbing me in the parking garage. Barely looked human. Twitching and shaking. Watch, like this."

He hunched forward, jerked his arms, and made his whole body spasm like something broken.

The executives exploded into laughter. My stomach turned over. The wine in my mouth went sour.

That's how Leo looked when I saw him last. Three days without sleep. Hands shaking so badly he couldn't hold his phone. Body moving in ways he couldn't control.

"They walk like zombies!" Another executive jumped up. I didn't even know his name. His whiskey sloshed over the rim. He shuffled across the floor with limp arms and dead eyes. "Like this! Brain-dead!"

More laughter. Louder. Other guests turned to watch.

Leo had carried groceries for Mrs. Garcia even when his hands shook. Leo had drawn cartoons for the apartment kids.

Leo had made me laugh with terrible jokes while Dad destroyed our kitchen.

"Police need to crack down harder," the nameless executive said, still swaying and grinning. "Lock them all up. Throw away the key. They're worthless parasites."

Parasites. Worthless.

The chandelier burned too bright. The room buzzed too loud. My pulse hammered in my throat like something trying to break free.

"I saw one yesterday!" Robert lurched forward, arms jerking wildly, legs dragging. "Stumbling around talking to invisible people. Arms flying everywhere like a broken puppet!"

The group howled, bent over their drinks, expensive suits flashing in crystal light.

David scratched at his arms frantically. His jacket slipped off one shoulder. "And they're always scratching! Like bugs crawling under their skin!"

He clawed at himself, grinned wide, and performed for the crowd. They roared with laughter. And then I heard it.

Margaret's laugh. Sharp. Clear. Cutting through all the other noise.

I turned my head. She stood right there next to David. That silver dress catching the light. Her head tilted back slightly as she laughed at her husband's performance.

She was laughing.

The woman who inspired me. The woman I'd taped to my wall. The woman who said success doesn't come from where you start. She was laughing at jokes about dying addicts.

My chest cracked open.

"Absolutely right," Robert said louder, drunk and confident. "They choose this life. Nobody forced them to shoot up. There's no excuse for being a junkie."

And then I saw him.

Leo.

Standing right behind them in the hoodie he died in. Face hollow. Body too thin. But still him. Still my little brother. His eyes locked on mine. Wide. Unbearably sad.

He didn't move. Didn't speak. Just stood there watching these people. Watching Margaret turn his pain into entertainment.

A burning smell hit me. Sharp. Acrid. Like when Dad passed out with a cigarette and almost killed us. But there was no smoke here. Just panic choking me. Just perfume and wine and laughter suffocating me.

"They're animals," the nameless man said, swaying. "No different than rabid dogs. Better to put them down."

Another executive raised his glass high. His arm passed straight through Leo like he wasn't even there.

"Here's to cleaning up the streets! Get rid of the garbage!"

Glasses clinked. Bodies jerked and twitched. Rich people in thousand-dollar suits playing at being broken.

Margaret laughed again. Lighter this time. Delighted. And Leo just stood there. Silent. Hollow. Watching the woman I'd admired mock everything he'd suffered through.

My hands started shaking. The wine glass slipped from my fingers. Cold. Slick. The chandelier light broke through the crystal into tiny rainbows across my palm.

The room swayed. Or I swayed. My heartbeat roared in my ears, drowning out everything except that sound.

Leo looked at me one last time. That same expression from childhood. Pure faith. Like his big sister could protect him from anything. But I hadn't protected him. I'd let him die alone.

And now Margaret Carrington, the woman who showed me the way out, was standing here laughing at people like him.

The glass slipped from my fingers. It hit marble. A sharp crack that sounded like a gunshot. Crystal exploded across white stone. Red wine sprayed everywhere.

The ballroom went silent. Conversations died mid-word. Heads turned. Fifty people. Maybe more. All staring at the woman who had just shattered glass at a black-tie event.

Leo vanished. I tasted copper. Blood from biting my tongue. Or maybe just rage crawling up my throat.

"MY BROTHER WAS NOT AN ANIMAL!"

The scream tore out of me. Three years of silence. Three years of grief. All of it exploding into crystal-lit air.

Every head snapped toward me. The executives stepped back. Their drunk grins melted away. Faces went pale.

"He was nineteen years old!" My voice cracked. "He was scared! And you people in your fancy suits don't know what it's like!"

Margaret's face remained smooth. Empty. Just watching me like I was a mildly interesting TV show.

"You don't know what it's like growing up in a house where your father drinks away the grocery money!" Words kept pouring out. I couldn't stop them. "You don't know what it's like choosing between food and medicine!"

David blinked, startled. "Miss Parker, perhaps—"

"You think they choose this life?" My voice grew shrill. Unstoppable. "You think a seven-year-old chooses to hide in the basement while his drunk father throws plates? You think a twelve-year-old chooses to go to school hungry because Daddy spent lunch money on whiskey?"

Jennifer pushed through the crowd, her face pale with horror.

But the wine had burned away every wall. Every defense I'd built for three years. My grief spilled out in front of Chicago's elite.

"Sometimes there's no choice!" I screamed. "Sometimes when you grow up with violence and fear and never enough money, substances are the only thing that stops the pain! Sometimes reality is too hard, and you'll take anything that makes you feel normal for five minutes!"

Silence. Complete silence. Three hundred successful professionals watching a McKinsey consultant unravel.

I looked straight at Margaret. She still hadn't moved. Hadn't blinked. Just stood there cold and perfect. Everything I'd wanted to become.

"Do you know what it's like watching someone you love fight a disease every day and lose?" My voice shook. "Do you know what it's like loving someone who's trying so hard to get sober while the world tells them they're worthless?"

Phones came out. Glowing screens pointed at me. Recording. Capturing Olivia Parker's life shattering like the glass at her feet.

"He wasn't a burden!" Mascara burned hot down my cheeks. "He wasn't choosing to be a problem! He was a human being born into hell, and he never had the chances you take for granted!"

My voice cracked completely.

"My brother could have been just like you if he'd had college funds and parents who stayed sober long enough to read him bedtime stories!"

"Ma'am." A security guard's voice cut through. "You need to calm down."

But I couldn't. I looked at Margaret one more time. Her face still blank. Still calculating. Like I was a business problem she was figuring out how to solve.

"He died believing I'd save him!" The sob ripped from my chest. "He believed that because I was the one who got out. I made it to college. Got the fancy job. And when he needed eight thousand dollars to stay alive, I said no!"

My voice broke into pieces.

"I said no because I was too busy protecting my precious reputation!"

The guards reached me just as my legs gave out. I collapsed on cold marble. My expensive dress pooled around me, surrounded by broken crystal and spilled wine.

Everything I'd built in Chicago lay there with me. Shattered.

Jennifer knelt down, her eyes shiny with tears. "Olivia, honey. Let's get you out of here."

But it was too late. Three hundred witnesses. Multiple videos already uploading. My McKinsey name tag clear in every shot. I'd just destroyed my career in the most public way possible.

I looked up one last time through tears and mascara. Margaret Carrington stood above me. Still untouched. Still perfect. Looking down at me lying in broken glass like I was exactly what she'd known from the beginning.

Trash.

Someone who didn't belong. Someone who'd never escape where they came from. And somewhere in my wine-soaked brain, I knew she was right.

I was exactly like my father, after all.

The next forty-eight hours blurred into shame and fallout.

Monday morning, I sat in a glass-walled conference room while McKinsey's senior partners played my breakdown on a big screen. The sound echoed in the sterile space. My voice screaming about Leo, my mascara running, the crystal glass shattering. Twelve people in expensive suits sat in silence, watching me unravel in high definition.

"This has been viewed over fifty thousand times," the managing partner said finally. His voice was calm in that way people use when they're about to ruin you. "Our biggest clients are calling about 'stability' and 'judgment.'"

Jennifer sat across from me, looking like she hadn't slept since the night of the event. Her face was drawn, her eyes older. "The Carrington account is gone," she said. "They've asked for another firm. Davidson Industries too. Premier Financial as well."

Three clients. Millions of dollars. Just gone. I sat frozen, staring at the screen. My own face looked back at me: red, wet, broken.

"We're going to have to let you go," the partner said. "Effective immediately. No severance. No references."

I nodded. What else could I do? I'd crossed every line. I'd made the whole firm look reckless. I'd probably just blacklisted myself from every consulting job in Chicago.

"I'm sorry," I whispered.

"So are we," he replied.

Jennifer walked me to my office while I packed up my things. Three years of a career fit into one cardboard box: two photos, a couple of coffee mugs, a plant I'd probably kill within a week.

"I'm really sorry, Olivia," she said as I cleared my desk. "I know you're carrying a lot, but I can't protect you from this."

"I know."

She hesitated. "Have you thought about getting help? For the drinking?"

The words hung between us, heavy. Everyone had seen the video. Everyone had seen the wine in my hand.

"I don't have a drinking problem," I said automatically. "I just had a bad night."

Her eyes softened, and somehow that hurt more than anger would have. "Okay," she said quietly. "Take care of yourself."

That night, I drove home in silence. My box of office junk sat on the passenger seat like evidence of failure.

Raymond was on the couch when I walked in, fully dressed at eleven at night, staring at his phone. His expression gave nothing away.

"How bad is it?" I asked, though my stomach already knew.

He held up his phone. The video had seventy thousand views. Comments scrolled faster than I could read: *McKinsey Consultant Has Epic Meltdown. Wine and Tears at the Peninsula. Consultant Breaks Down Over Dead Brother.*

"Shit," I whispered, dropping into the chair across from him.

"Yeah." His voice was flat. "Shit."

I opened the bottle waiting on the counter and poured myself a glass. My hands were still shaking from the adrenaline crash. Wine was the only thing that made them steady.

"This will blow over," I said, drinking deeply. "People forget fast. By next week, nobody will care."

Raymond finally looked at me. His eyes were hollow and heavy. "Will they? Because this isn't the first time, Olivia."

I frowned. "What do you mean?"

"The charity gala where you argued with the mayor's wife about homeless policies. The wine tasting where you cried for twenty minutes about your father."

I shook my head. "Those were different."

"Were they?" He gestured to my glass. "Because all of them had one thing in common."

"I wasn't drunk," I snapped. "Tipsy at worst. There's a difference."

Raymond laughed once, sharp and humorless. "You think there's a difference between what you do and what your father did?"

The words slapped me. "Don't you dare. I'm nothing like him."

"Aren't you?" He stood up, walked into the kitchen, and came back with three empty bottles. He lined them up on the coffee table, neat in a row. "I found these in the recycling. From this weekend."

I stared at them. "So what? I entertain clients. I host dinners."

"When was the last time you had a dinner party?"

I couldn't answer. Because I hadn't. Not in months. Every drop had been mine, alone, poured late at night while Raymond was gone or when I couldn't sleep.

"When was the last day you didn't drink?" he asked.

Silence. Because even on my "good" days, I had at least one glass with dinner. Usually more.

"When was the last time we had sex and you were sober?"

My throat closed. The answer sat there, ugly and undeniable. Months. Maybe longer. I needed wine to relax enough, to shut off the voice in my head that told me I wasn't enough.

"You're exaggerating," I muttered, but even I could hear how weak it sounded.

"Am I?" His voice was calm now, almost too calm. "Because I've been watching you for two years. Watching you drink before every event. Watching you get nervous if a restaurant doesn't serve alcohol. Watching you pour wine into your coffee mug at home when you think I don't notice."

He sat across from me again, his voice soft but sharper than anything else he'd said.

"I've been watching you turn into someone I don't know. Someone who can't get through a day without it. Someone who fights every time I bring it up."

"I function perfectly well," I said. My voice sounded too bright, as if I were trying to convince both of us. "Better than perfectly. Wine helps me at my job. It helps me connect with clients. It helps me—"

"Helps you destroy your career in front of three hundred people?"

His words dropped between us like a hammer. I couldn't dodge them.

"That was an anomaly," I said quickly. "I was under pressure, and they were saying horrible things about Leo, and—"

"And you were drunk," Raymond cut in. His voice was flat but shaking. "Just like you've been drunk at every important event this past year. Just like you're drunk right now."

I looked down at my wine glass. Empty. When had I finished it? I didn't remember lifting it to my mouth.

"I love you," Raymond said, and his voice cracked on the word. "But I can't watch you kill yourself with expensive wine while calling it culture. I can't keep being part of it."

"You're not enabling anything," I said. "You're—"

"I'm what? Supporting your wine education? Helping you 'discover' new varietals? Taking you to tastings where you drink three times as much as everyone else?" He stood, pacing. His footsteps were sharp against the floor. "That's exactly what enablers do, Olivia. I've been making it easier for you to drink by pretending it's sophisticated."

The room tilted slightly. Maybe from the wine. Maybe from exhaustion. Maybe from everything crashing down at once.

"What do you want me to say?" I asked. My voice came out small.

"I want you to say you have a problem," he said. "I want you to say you need help. I want you to admit that that night wasn't about pressure or Leo or mean executives. It was about a woman who can't control her drinking having a public breakdown."

"I can control my drinking."

"No, you can't. And neither could my father. And neither could your father. And if you don't get help, you're going to end up just like both of them."

He grabbed his jacket from the back of the couch, the one he'd been keeping there since he started sleeping in the living room.

"Where are you going?" I asked.

"Home. To my apartment. I can't stay here anymore, Olivia. I can't watch this happen."

"Raymond, please—"

"When you're ready to admit you have a problem, call me. Until then, I'm done pretending that loving you is enough to save you from yourself."

He walked to the door, then turned back one last time.

"Your brother died from addiction, Olivia. Don't let his death mean nothing by following the same path."

Then he left. He walked out of my apartment and out of my life while I stood in the middle of the living room, surrounded by empty bottles. My hands were shaking with rage. Or maybe terror.

Because everything he'd said was true. And I hated him for seeing it. I hated myself for proving him right by immediately reaching for another bottle to numb the void he left behind.

The wine tasted like tears. Like broken promises. Like the slow crumbling of everything I'd built in Chicago. But it worked. For a few hours, it made the pain bearable. And that was all that mattered anymore.

Chapter Eight

The Unemployable

THREE MONTHS AFTER MY life blew up in front of Chicago's business elite, I was still pretending I could fix it.

Mornings became a kind of denial ritual. My phone alarm at 6:47, the same time every day, jolted me awake to the sound of the upstairs neighbors fighting about rent. I checked my phone for messages that never came. Not from employers. Not from Raymond. His number was still at the top of my recent calls list like a ghost, but I hadn't heard his voice since the day he left.

I showered with the expensive shampoo I couldn't afford to replace but also couldn't throw away. I rotated through one of the three blazers that still fit, though each hung looser now. Stress had eaten away at both my appetite and savings.

I'd called Raymond twice that first week. Straight to voice-mail each time. His voice sounded cheerful and professional, like nothing had happened: *You've reached Raymond Photography, please leave a message...* I never did. What was I going to say? That I missed him? That he'd been right? That I was drowning without him but still couldn't stop drinking?

Last week, I drove past his building and saw a new name taped to the mailbox. Mr. Grant. Raymond had moved out. No forwarding address. He'd erased himself from my geography as cleanly as he'd erased himself from my life.

Coffee had become survival. Too much sugar to mask the metallic tang of anxiety that seemed to linger on my tongue all day. Seventeen new rejection emails since yesterday, each one saying the same thing:

Thank you for your interest... while your qualifications are impressive, we've decided to move forward with candidates who better align with our company culture.

Company culture. Code for: *we Googled you and saw the video.*

The Peninsula Hotel breakdown was at 134,000 views now. Someone had even clipped my voice screaming *"MY BROTHER WAS NOT AN ANIMAL!"* and turned it into a TikTok audio. Teenagers were layering it over videos of spilled coffee and flat tires. #OliviaMeltdown had thousands of likes. My ruined life, recycled as comedy.

I closed my laptop and poured wine into my coffee mug. Not because I wanted to drink at nine in the morning, but because my hands were shaking too badly to hold it steady without help. The good bottles were long gone. Now it was whatever was cheapest at the corner store. But wine in a mug before noon still felt "sophisticated." European, I told myself. Not desperate. Not Dad.

That lie mattered. Even if I was the only one who believed it.

The Henderson & Associates interview was supposed to be different.

I'd found them through a temp agency that worked with people "between opportunities." Translation: people with blemishes on their records. Their office was in a converted warehouse in a part of town I'd never been, but it felt professional enough. Clean lobby, receptionist who smiled.

I'd managed twenty-two hours sober. Unless you counted the glass of Pinot I had with breakfast. Just enough to calm the buzzing in my chest. Just enough to steady my hands so I could look normal when I walked into the room.

James Henderson looked exactly like his LinkedIn photo. Fifty or so, kind eyes behind wire glasses, rumpled suit, bookshelves full of business strategy texts. A chipped coffee mug that said *World's Okayest Dad*. He looked human. Safe. Like maybe he'd look past the video and see me.

"Your McKinsey background is exactly what we need," he said, scanning my resume. "Market optimization, supply chains. That's our bread and butter, but we don't have anyone with your level of experience."

For half an hour, I felt like myself again. We talked pricing strategies and client relationships. He nodded when I explained how I'd helped Fortune 500 companies streamline operations. For thirty minutes, I wasn't the girl from the viral meltdown. I was the consultant who knew how to fix things.

"I think you'd be an excellent fit for our senior consultant role," Henderson said, and my chest lifted with something I hadn't felt in months: hope. "Salary range ninety to one hundred twenty thousand. Full benefits, four weeks' vacation. We're more like a family than a corporation."

Ninety thousand. Not McKinsey money, but enough. Enough to get my life back. Enough to stop hiding wine in coffee mugs and to believe I could rebuild.

"That sounds wonderful," I said, careful not to sound too desperate. "When would you like me to start?"

"Let me just pull up your references, and we can talk next steps." He reached for his laptop with the easy confidence of someone doing something routine.

The moment his fingers touched the keyboard, my stomach dropped.

I watched his face change in real time. Enthusiasm faded to confusion. Confusion tightened into concern. His mouth opened, then closed again. The faint sound of audio started. My voice, screaming before he scrambled to mute it.

The silence stretched, heavy as stone. Then he turned the screen toward me.

YouTube.

The Peninsula Hotel ballroom, frozen in a thumbnail. My face mid-scream, mascara streaked like war paint, surrounded by men in suits leaning away as if I were radioactive. The view counter ticked up right in front of us: 134,247 and climbing.

The comments were the same wasteland I already knew by heart. *Psycho consultant loses it. This is why women shouldn't be in business. Guess McKinsey hires addicts now.*

"Is this you?" Henderson asked. His voice was quiet and careful, like he was asking me to identify a body.

I could have lied. Said it was someone else, a lookalike, a case of mistaken identity. But my McKinsey name tag was right there on the screen. My name in the title for anyone to see.

"Yes," I whispered. "But I can explain—"

"I don't think that's necessary." He closed the laptop with the deliberate care of someone ending a conversation while trying to be kind. "We'll be in touch."

We both knew what that meant. The interview was over. The job was gone. Seventy-five thousand dollars, four weeks of vacation, the fragile hope of rebuilding. It all evaporated in the time it took a YouTube video to load.

I stood on unsteady legs, shook his hand, and walked out of his office pretending I still had dignity. I made it to the hallway before my throat closed up.

The elevator ride down felt like descending into hell. Each floor was another reminder that I wasn't that consultant anymore. I was someone else now. Someone unemployable not because I lacked skill, but because the internet had branded me with ninety seconds of grief and rage that would follow me forever.

In the brushed steel doors, I saw her again. The girl from the video. Same face, only thinner now. More hollow around the eyes. Like someone had been erasing me, line by line, from the inside out.

And then Leo was there.

Sitting in one of the leather chairs by the windows like he belonged there, hoodie zipped to his chin, hair falling into his eyes. Younger than the morgue photos, older than the boy who built blanket forts. Somewhere in between.

He didn't look at me at first. Just stared through the glass, shaking his head as if he were watching a movie where the heroine kept making the wrong choice. His lips moved, but no sound came out, like he was arguing with someone I couldn't see.

When his eyes finally met mine, it wasn't anger I saw. It was heartbreak. Pure, crushing disappointment that cut deeper than any accusation could.

"I know," I whispered. The receptionist looked up sharply, probably wondering who I was talking to.

Leo nodded, slow and solemn, like he'd heard the apology I didn't know how to give. Then, he was gone.

I stood alone in the lobby, crying in front of strangers about a job I'd never get and a brother I'd never save.

By the time I got to my car, my hands were shaking so hard I could barely turn the key. I drove home on autopilot, the city a blur of traffic lights and honking horns. The wine was waiting in my apartment. I drank until Henderson's disappointed face and Leo's sad eyes blurred together into one long nightmare.

But they always came back. Every morning. Every rejection email. Every reminder that I had become unemployable in a city where reputation was everything.

And the wine helped less every day. But it was still the only thing that helped at all.

Apartment hunting was like walking through the stages of my own decline.

At first, I looked at studios in Lincoln Park. Small, but respectable. Murphy beds, tiny kitchens, but addresses you could still say out loud without shame. Places that made me feel like maybe I still belonged among the people I used to work with.

But as the rejections piled up and my savings drained, I expanded my search to areas farther out: Logan Square, Wicker Park, Humboldt Park. Neighborhoods agents called "up and coming," code for "cheap enough that people with choices stay away."

The call came on a sweltering July afternoon while I was halfway through an application for an entry-level consulting job that paid less than half of what I used to make.

"Ms. Parker, I hope you're doing well."

It was Tom Brennan, my landlord. I'd lived in his building for three years and had never once heard his voice. All communication went through the property company. A personal call meant personal trouble.

"I'm fine," I lied. "What's going on?"

"Well, property values in Lincoln Park have increased significantly. Market rates are running about thirty percent higher than your current lease."

Thirty percent. The number hit me like a punch.

"So if you'd like to renew, we'd need to adjust your rent to thirty-seven hundred monthly. I know it's steep, but comparable units are going for more."

I set my wine glass carefully on the coffee table. The same overpriced piece I'd bought when Raymond moved in, back when I thought expensive furniture proved you were the kind of person who deserved nice things.

Now it was just a reminder that I wasn't.

"Thirty-seven hundred dollars," I repeated, my voice thin. My thumb opened my banking app while Tom kept talking about market conditions and comparable properties, his voice a polite drone I barely registered.

$4,127.84. The number glowed back at me like a death sentence.

At my current rent, I had maybe six weeks left. At the new rate, maybe four if I stopped eating and stopped buying wine.

But wine wasn't optional anymore. Wine was what made the rejection emails tolerable. Wine was what let me sleep through nights when the future spun like a broken record inside my skull.

"Can I think about it?" I asked.

"Of course. Just let me know by August first so we can list it if you're not staying."

After he hung up, I sat in my kitchen staring at everything I was about to lose.

The lake view that used to make me feel like I'd made it, sitting with my morning coffee, planning big days. The granite countertops where I'd prepared elaborate dinners for colleagues who now pretended not to know me. The dining table where Raymond and I had shared bottles of wine more expensive than some people's groceries, planning trips to Napa, discussing partnership as if it were inevitable.

All of it was about to become someone else's life.

I opened a bottle of Sauvignon Blanc and started scrolling through Craigslist for apartments I could afford with no job and a savings account shrinking by the day.

The listings read like a map of my dwindling prospects.

$2,500 studios in trendy neighborhoods where I could still pretend nothing had changed. $1,800 one-bedrooms in places where I'd need to explain why someone with my degree lived there. $1,200 studios in neighborhoods where no one asked questions because they had their own problems.

Each lower price felt like another step down a staircase I'd never imagined I'd be on.

The place I finally settled on was in Logan Square, wedged between a laundromat that ran industrial dryers twenty-four hours a day and a store selling phone cards to people who couldn't get credit. Six hundred square feet that smelled like old cigarettes and decades of other people's disappointments.

But it was $1,200 a month. Three months of survival if I found work soon. Three months if I cut everything else down to the bare minimum.

Moving day came on a Saturday so hot the asphalt softened under my feet. I'd spent the last two weeks selling off my life one item at a time, each sale feeling like cutting off a limb.

The dining table went first.

"How much for the dining set?" asked a young woman who looked exactly like me three years ago. Professional clothes, steady paycheck optimism, the glow of someone building a life instead of dismantling one.

"Four hundred," I said, though I'd paid twelve hundred when I thought I was building something permanent.

"Would you take three-fifty?"

I wanted to explain: this table had hosted dinner parties with colleagues now climbing ladders I'd fallen off. Raymond and I had planned our future over wine and pasta at these chairs. It was everything I'd worked for, everything I was losing.

Instead, I said, "Three-fifty is fine."

She paid in cash. Her boyfriend helped her load it into their SUV. They drove off laughing about something, probably planning their first dinner party, excited about the future they were still sure of.

I stood in my emptying living room holding three hundred and fifty dollars. Ten days of rent and tried to remember when I'd stopped being someone who bought furniture and started being someone who sold it.

The couch went next. Then the coffee table. Then the art I'd bought to prove I understood culture. Each transaction felt like a tiny funeral for the person I used to be.

By moving day, everything I owned fit into the back of a rental truck that smelled like other people's desperate relocations.

My first night in the Logan Square apartment, I sat on an air mattress surrounded by boxes I didn't have the energy to open. The windows faced an alley where reggaeton thumped too loudly, and two people argued about money in rapid-fire Spanish.

This was what failure looked like up close. This was where you landed when the internet made you unemployable, and pride became too expensive to afford.

"Small place."

I nearly dropped my wine glass. Dad was sitting in the folding chair I'd picked up at a thrift store for fifteen dollars, the only other piece of furniture I had.

He looked different. Younger. Not the bloated, exhausted man who'd died in a hospital but the version from old Polaroids. Maybe forty, maybe still believing he could regain control, still making promises he thought he could keep.

"It's temporary," I said, though we both knew it was a lie. This apartment was exactly what I could afford now, and nothing in my inbox suggested it would change soon.

Dad looked around at the boxes, the bare walls, the single folding chair. "I lived in places like this," he said quietly. "After Linda kicked me out the first time."

"Before she let you come back?"

"Before I convinced her I was different. Before we all pretended the promises would stick this time." He stared at the wine glass in my hand. "You remember what you used to say when you were little?"

I shook my head.

"You'd say, 'Daddy, why do you drink the medicine that makes you sick?'" His voice went soft, almost tender. "Smart kid. Saw right through all the excuses."

My chest tightened. "I don't remember that."

"Do you still see through them, princess? The excuses?"

I wanted to tell him this was different. That I was drinking because of unemployment, because of stress, not because I was like him. That wine was sophisticated and temporary, not desperate and permanent.

But I was sitting on an air mattress in a studio apartment that smelled like cigarettes, drinking wine out of a coffee mug because I'd sold my wine glasses, and my hands were trembling from withdrawal even though I'd had three glasses in the past hour.

I blinked, and he was gone. Just me. Alone in six hundred square feet of everything I'd never wanted to be.

I finished the bottle and opened another one. Thinking was dangerous. Wine was the only thing that made the thinking stop.

The vodka discovery came during a week in August when everything felt impossible. I was out of wine money, down to ten dollars in my checking account, and still pretending I could stretch it further than it would go.

I stood in the liquor aisle at Jewel-Osco, doing math as if my job depended on it. The lights above buzzed loud and flat, making everything look harsher. People pushed carts around me with real dinners inside them (vegetables, pasta, meat) like they belonged to some other world I'd already fallen out of.

Kendall-Jackson Chardonnay: $15.99. Seven hundred and fifty milliliters. Twelve percent alcohol. The one I'd been buying, the one that felt safe, was out of reach now.

Smirnoff Vodka: $8.99. Same size bottle. Forty percent alcohol.

I ran the numbers again and again. Vodka gave me three times the alcohol for half the price. It was efficient. It was logical. The kind of calculation I used to get praised for at McKinsey.

But vodka was Dad's drink. Vodka was dive bars in the afternoon. Vodka was the difference between calling it sophisticated and admitting you were just a drunk.

Wine had let me pretend. Wine had a script. Dinners, charity galas, networking. It sounded civilized when I said it out loud.

I checked my phone again. Balance: $10.47.

Boundaries didn't matter anymore. I set the vodka in my cart next to bread and peanut butter. Three nights of meals, and I felt my shoulders drop, lighter somehow, like I'd stopped lying to myself.

At the checkout, the girl with purple hair didn't even blink. She'd probably seen it all already. She scanned the bottle like it was nothing. "Fourteen thirty-seven," she said, not looking at me.

I handed over fifteen dollars. Almost all I had left and walked out of the store feeling like I'd crossed a line that couldn't be uncrossed.

The first sip at home was fire. It burned down my throat, nothing like the soft warmth of wine. This was sharp, chemical, something that made me cough and blink hard. But it worked.

It worked fast.

Within ten minutes, the noise in my head eased: the emails, the rejection, the video that wouldn't stop following me. It all dulled around the edges. The apartment didn't feel so small. My life didn't feel so unbearable.

I floated in that numb place where problems could wait.

"Smart about money?"

The voice came from the kitchen. I turned, and there was Leo, leaning in the doorway with his arms crossed. His face carried that look he used to give me when I nagged him about choices.

He didn't speak again. Just stared. His lips moved like he was trying to tell me something in a language I couldn't understand anymore. Then he lifted his arms. The purple track marks glared at me, the same ones I'd seen in the morgue photos. He pointed at the vodka bottle, then at his arms, then back at me.

Not accusing. Just showing me.

"It's not the same," I whispered. My own voice sounded weak.

His eyes didn't change. Still steady. Still sad.

"It's different," I said louder. "You used heroin. I drink. Everyone drinks."

But he was already fading, gone before I could convince either of us.

I poured another drink anyway. The pain in front of me was real. The consequences belonged to tomorrow. And tomorrow felt far away when the fire in my glass made everything blur.

Running into Kerri was like stepping straight into a mine I knew was buried but had forgotten to avoid.

It was Wednesday at eleven in the morning. I was at the grocery store with a basket that told the truth: cheap vodka, frozen dinners, one banana I'd thrown in to look like I still cared.

"Olivia? Olivia Parker?"

Her voice froze me in place.

I turned and saw her. Kerri. Tailored blazer, expensive bag, posture that exuded confidence. She looked exactly like I used to look, back when I thought the world had room for me in it.

She'd started at McKinsey half a year after I did. I'd shown her the ropes, taught her how to talk to clients, where to sit in meetings, and how to survive travel. We'd celebrated promotions with champagne, back when I still had a career to celebrate.

Now she stared at me like I was wreckage on the side of the road.

"Kerri! Hi!" My voice came out too high, too bright, like I was acting instead of speaking. "How are things at the office?"

"Great. Really great." Her eyes flicked to my basket. The vodka sat there in plain sight, impossible to hide among the frozen dinners and sad groceries. "I just made senior associate."

Senior associate. The job that should have been mine. The promotion I'd been working toward before I fell apart in front of three hundred people. That title, that salary, that office. All the things that belonged to me if I hadn't fallen apart.

"That's wonderful," I said, trying to sound happy for her instead of crushed by my own failure. "You deserve it."

"Thanks." Kerri smiled, but it wasn't genuine. It was careful, like she wanted to be kind but also wanted to escape. "Are you... how are you doing? Everyone asks about you at the office."

I'll bet they do. Probably whispering about how far the golden girl had fallen. Using me as a cautionary tale for new hires. This is what happens when you don't keep it together.

"I'm doing great," I lied, smooth from practice. "I'm consulting independently now. More flexibility. Better work-life balance."

The lie rolled off my tongue too easily. The truth... that I was broke, unemployable, drinking vodka before breakfast just to keep my hands steady... was something I could never say out loud to Kerri. Not Kerri, who used to look at me like I was worth admiring.

"That sounds amazing." Her tone had that polite edge. The one people use when they don't believe you but don't want to call you a liar. "Independent consulting must be so rewarding."

"It is," I said, gripping my basket tighter to hide the tremor in my hands. "I'm working with several Fortune 500 companies on supply chain optimization."

Another lie. I hadn't worked with anyone in months. I couldn't even land an interview at a small firm. But Kerri's professional smile demanded I pretend.

"Olivia, you look..." She hesitated, searching for the right word. Because I looked terrible. Hair pulled back in a messy ponytail, makeup smeared from shaky hands, clothes sagging from the weight I'd lost. Stress and vodka had taken their toll.

"Different," she finally said. The kindest word she could find.

"Well, you know how consulting is," I said quickly, filling the silence. "Lots of travel, long hours. Doesn't leave much time for..." I waved a hand at myself, as if this wreck of a body was just the price of being busy.

"Of course." Kerri nodded, already pulling away. "Well, I should let you get back to your shopping. It was so good to see you."

Her voice was artificially bright. My lie was feigned strength. We both played along because the truth was unbearable.

"You too," I said. "Say hi to everyone at the office for me."

"I will." She backed away toward the organic produce, moving quickly as if I carried something contagious. "Take care of yourself, Olivia."

And then she was gone.

I stood in the discount aisle with my basket full of proof that I was exactly what people thought I was: a fallen star. A warning.

I could already hear the story she'd tell later at happy hour. *I ran into Olivia Parker at the grocery store. She looked awful. Said she was consulting on her own, but she was buying cheap vodka at eleven in the morning. So sad.*

Sad. Pitying. And true.

I finished shopping in a haze, avoiding the cashier's gaze. He'd seen me enough times buying vodka too early to know the truth already. My hands shook on the steering wheel the entire drive home.

The vodka was waiting in my studio that still smelled like cigarettes. I drank until Kerri's face stopped looping in my mind, that polite smile that said she was glad to escape me.

But it always came back. Every morning. Every rejection. Every reminder that I'd gone from respected to pitied.

The vodka helped less every day, but it was all I had left.

By the end of summer, I'd received forty-three rejections. Pride was gone. It had become just another luxury.

The last interview had been at a nonprofit helping homeless families find housing. Even they didn't want me. My "history" was too much.

So I started scrolling through jobs that didn't care who I used to be. Jobs that didn't ask for references or explanations. Retail. Service. Twelve dollars an hour if I was lucky.

McKinsey felt like another lifetime. Now I was just someone trying to buy time.

Chapter Nine

From McKinsey to Nordstrom

B Y SEPTEMBER, PRIDE HAD turned into a luxury I couldn't afford.

The Nordstrom application was humiliating in a painfully ordinary way. Filling in boxes about employment history, smoothing over gaps with phrases like "pursuing new opportunities," pretending four months of unemployment was a choice. Once, my resume had been a ticket into boardrooms and client dinners. Now it was a liability I kept trying to disguise.

But Nordstrom needed seasonal help for the holidays, and seasonal help meant bodies. People who could smile, show up on time, and fold clothes without stealing them. No one cared if I'd once managed million-dollar accounts or worn designer suits to client dinners. They just wanted someone who could keep sweaters stacked neatly on a shelf.

The interview was with Susan, a woman who looked like she'd been in retail longer than I'd been alive. Her face carried the weary patience of someone who'd interviewed hundreds of people who'd ended up here for reasons too messy to ask about.

"Any customer service experience?" she asked, glancing at my application without much interest.

"Some," I said. It was true if you squinted and counted consulting as customer service. "I'm good with people."

"Can you work evenings and weekends?"

"Absolutely." I could work any hour they wanted. I didn't have a social life. My only calendar was bottles of vodka and the messages from Linda I couldn't bear to answer.

Susan nodded, scribbling something on my application. "This is the Water Tower location. Flagship store. We get a... certain clientele." She said it like a warning. "Corporate executives. Society types. People who expect service."

My stomach dropped. Water Tower. The nice Nordstrom. The one where women like Margaret Carrington shopped.

"Is that a problem?" Susan was watching me now, as if she'd caught something in my expression.

"No," I said quickly. "That's fine."

"Good. Because some people can't handle it. The customers here can be demanding. Entitled. They know what they want, and they expect you to provide it with a smile."

I forced myself to nod, to look confident, as if I weren't already thinking about all the McKinsey clients who probably shopped here. All the people from that world who might recognize me.

But what were the odds? Chicago was a big city. Nordstrom employed hundreds of people across dozens of departments. I could disappear into the racks of clothes and never see anyone I knew.

That's what I told myself.

"Twelve dollars an hour," Susan continued. "Employee discount, flexible scheduling. Sound good?"

Twelve dollars an hour. At McKinsey, I used to make more than that in the time it took me to order lunch. But twelve was still better than zero, and zero had been my salary for four long months.

"Perfect," I said.

She handed me a name tag and a black polo shirt. It felt like a costume, like something I was borrowing from a life that wasn't mine.

"Welcome to the Nordstrom family."

The first days weren't as bad as I'd braced myself for.

They stuck me in women's clothing on the second floor. Designer section. My job was simple: point customers toward sizes, hang things back up, clean out dressing rooms. It was brainless, which was good, because most mornings I showed up still tasting vodka. The water bottle in my locker wasn't filled with water, but no one asked.

My coworkers were college kids saving up for textbooks and retirees who needed something to fill their hours. People with normal problems and normal families who talked about classes, bills, and grandkids without shame.

On my second day, I met Monica, my supervisor. She'd worked the designer section for six years and knew every regular by name.

"You'll get used to them," she said while we were restocking a rack of silk blouses. "The ladies who lunch. They come in every week, sometimes twice. Spend more on a single dress than I make in a month."

"Anyone I should know about?" I asked, trying to sound casual.

Monica laughed. "Oh honey, where do I start? There's Mrs. Whitmore. She never buys anything under a thousand dollars. The Bancroft sisters. They try on everything and buy nothing. And the Carringtons." She said the name with a mix of reverence and exhaustion. "Margaret Carrington. She's here at least once a week. Always knows exactly what she wants. Tips well if you're helpful."

My hands froze on the hanger I was holding.

"Carrington?" I managed to keep my voice steady. "Like the media company?"

"That's the one. Margaret's the CEO's wife. Oh. Actually, she is the CEO? I can't remember exactly. Either way, serious money. Serious taste." Monica glanced at me. "You okay? You look like you've seen a ghost."

"I'm fine," I said. "Just... I think I know that name from somewhere."

"Probably the news. They're always in the society pages: galas, charity events, that kind of thing." Monica moved on to another rack. "Anyway, if you see her, be extra attentive. Management loves her. Corporate VIP account."

I nodded, my throat too tight to respond.

Margaret Carrington. Here. Once a week.

The woman who'd watched me scream about my dead brother in front of three hundred people. Who'd seen security carry me out like garbage. Who probably told that story at dinner parties as an amusing anecdote about the consultant who'd lost her mind.

And now I'd be helping her find dresses, fetching her sizes, smiling while she looked through me like I was part of the furniture.

"You sure you're okay?" Monica asked again. "You look pale."

"Low blood sugar," I lied. "I'll grab something from the break room."

I walked away before she could ask more questions. I made it to the bathroom and locked myself in a stall. My hands were shaking. My heart was pounding so hard I could feel it in my throat.

I should quit. Walk out right now. Find another job, any job, somewhere Margaret Carrington would never shop. But I couldn't afford to quit. Couldn't afford to be picky. I had sixty-three dollars in my bank account and rent due in two weeks.

So I stood there in that bathroom stall, breathing through the panic, telling myself it would be fine. Chicago was a big city. Nordstrom was a big store. The odds of her walking into my specific department on my specific shift were basically zero.

That's what I told myself. I believed it for exactly twelve days.

There was something oddly calming about the work once I stopped thinking about Margaret: folding clothes, organizing racks, helping a woman find a dress for her daughter's wedding. It kept my hands busy, kept my mind from running too far into dark corners.

My coworkers were easy to be around. I learned to smile and keep my answers vague when they asked what I used to do. "Transitioning between careers." "Exploring new opportunities." They probably guessed I was divorced or laid off from some dull job. Nobody would have guessed that six months earlier, I was sitting across from Fortune 500 executives, ordering bottles of wine that cost more than their rent.

For almost two weeks, I believed I could do this: show up, clock out, collect a paycheck. Start again from the bottom.

Then, on a Tuesday afternoon in late September, Monica grabbed my arm.

"Heads up," she said quietly. "Margaret Carrington just walked in. Ground floor, heading for the escalators."

My stomach turned to ice.

"I can take her," Monica offered. "If you want to work the stock room for a bit—"

"No." My voice came out steadier than I felt. "I'm fine. I can handle it."

Monica looked at me like she didn't quite believe me, but she nodded and went back to folding scarves.

I kept my head down, focused on arranging a display of fall sweaters. I told myself that even if Margaret came to the second floor, even if she walked through the designer section, she wouldn't remember me.

Six months had passed. I looked different now. Thinner. Tired. Hair pulled back instead of styled, black polo and khakis instead of tailored suits.

I was invisible. Just another retail worker in a store full of them. That's what I told myself right up until I heard her voice.

"Excuse me, could you help me find something?"

I turned around. And there she was.

Margaret Carrington. Standing three feet away, looking directly at me. For half a second, I thought maybe I'd gotten lucky. Maybe she didn't recognize me. Maybe I really was invisible.

Then her eyes narrowed. Just slightly. Like she was trying to place where she'd seen me before. And I watched the exact moment she remembered.

Her expression didn't change much. Just a small shift, a flicker of recognition followed by something that might have been satisfaction.

"Olivia Parker," she said. Not a question. A fact. "From the Peninsula Hotel."

The words landed like a punch. I felt every head nearby turn toward me. Monica glanced up from the register, already frowning.

"I'm sorry?" I managed, though my voice betrayed me.

"You're the consultant from the Peninsula Hotel," Margaret said. Her voice was softer now, but no less sharp. "The McKinsey consultant who had the... breakdown. At the networking event. You screamed about your brother."

The networking event. That was her polite phrase for the night I set fire to my own life in front of Chicago's elite.

"I think you're mistaken," I whispered, my denial weak even to my own ears.

"No." Her certainty was absolute, the kind of certainty that money and status provide from birth. "It's definitely you. Olivia Parker. I remember you from the event."

Other customers were staring now. The kind of women who shopped at Water Tower Nordstrom, who probably remembered the viral video that had been played and replayed until my face became a meme. And now here I was, folding their clothes, fetching their sizes for twelve dollars an hour.

"Is everything all right?" Monica appeared at my side, sensing trouble even if she didn't know why.

"Everything's fine," Margaret said with a bright, brittle smile that told everyone it wasn't. "I was just saying hello to an old… acquaintance."

But she didn't move on. She kept staring at me like I was an exhibit behind glass, like she was studying a warning sign about what happened when someone from her world fell. Her gaze lingered on my thinner frame, my tired face, cataloging the collapse.

"I should let you get back to work," she said eventually. But she didn't leave. She was savoring this, watching the woman who'd once been her equal reduced to retail labor.

"Actually," she added, sliding her phone out of her handbag, "could you help me find this dress? I saw it online." She held the screen toward me, and I nodded even though my hands were shaking too hard to focus on the picture.

"Of course," I managed. "Let me check our inventory."

I walked her through the racks, pulling dresses, pretending to care about fabric and fit while she peppered me with small talk that felt like paper cuts.

"So how long have you been here?" she asked, her tone syrupy with false interest. "It must be quite a change from consulting."

"A few months," I lied smoothly. "I'm taking time to explore different opportunities."

"How interesting," she said, the words hollow, her tone sharp with judgment. "And your family? How are they handling... everything?"

Everything. The viral video. The firing. The humiliation that lived online forever.

"They're fine," I said. Another lie. Linda was leaving voicemails every day, her voice raw with worry. But Margaret didn't need the truth.

"I'm sure they're very proud," she said. The fake kindness in her voice cut deeper than outright mockery ever could.

I found her size and walked her to the dressing rooms. She tried on three dresses, turning for my opinion like we were girlfriends shopping together instead of what we really were: a woman reveling in my ruin and the woman whose ruin she was enjoying.

"I'll take this one," she decided finally, holding out a black cocktail dress that cost more than I'd make in two weeks. "It's for a charity gala next month. You know how these events are."

Once, I would have known exactly what she meant. Now, I just nodded and carried the dress to the register.

As I rang it up, Margaret leaned across the counter, her voice lowering as if she was confiding something generous.

"You know," she said, "David felt awful about what happened at the Peninsula. He didn't realize you had such a personal connection to the matter."

The matter. My brother's overdose reduced to a policy debate.

"It's fine," I said, though the words scraped my throat raw.

"He wanted me to tell you... if you needed help, resources... there are programs for people facing challenges."

Challenges. The polite word for addict. For unemployable drunk. For me.

"Thank you," I said, handing her the shopping bag. "That's very kind."

She lingered a moment longer, studying me with an expression I couldn't read: pity, satisfaction, maybe both.

"Take care of yourself, Olivia," she said finally. "I hope things work out for you."

Then she walked away, leaving me behind the register with trembling hands and the certainty that she was already rehearsing the story she'd tell at her next dinner party: how she'd spotted the fallen McKinsey consultant at Nordstrom, ringing up her dress.

I muttered something to Monica about needing the restroom and walked as calmly as I could to the break room. My water bottle was waiting in my locker. I drank half the vodka in three quick swallows. The burn was both punishment and relief.

When I came back out, Margaret was gone. But Monica was waiting. I knew the look before she opened her mouth: the careful, uncomfortable face of someone sent to deliver bad news.

"Corporate called," she said gently. "They've decided to end your employment effective immediately."

Of course they had. Margaret Carrington had made a phone call. Thirty seconds of conversation, and I was fired.

I nodded and went back to my locker. I packed my few things while the other associates watched with curiosity, probably wondering what I'd done wrong. None of them would have guessed the truth. That I wasn't fired for stealing, or being late, or breaking the rules.

I was fired for being someone who'd once mattered, someone who'd fallen too far and dared to show up here.

The drive home was a blur of streetlights and vodka and the slow, crushing realization that I'd just lost the only income I'd had in months. I pulled into the parking lot of my apartment and sat there for twenty minutes, staring at the steering wheel, taking small sips from the water bottle, and trying to figure out what to do next.

When I looked up, Leo was standing outside the car. Not slumped in the passenger seat like before. Not the hollow version from the morgue photos.

He was standing in front of my headlights, hands shoved in his hoodie pockets, head tilted back like he was looking at stars. The same way he used to stand in our driveway when he was twelve, thirteen, fourteen. Before everything went wrong.

I could see him perfectly in the glow of the lights. The kid who used to drag me outside at night to show me constellations he'd learned in science class. Who'd point up and name them all. Orion, Cassiopeia, the Big Dipper, like he was giving me a tour of somewhere I'd never been.

"That one's Ursa Major," he'd say, so serious. So proud he'd remembered. "The Great Bear."

And I'd squint at the mess of stars and pretend I could see it too.

"Do you see it, Livvy?" he'd ask. "The bear?"

"Yeah," I'd lie. "I see it."

And he'd smile like I'd given him something precious. Like my attention was worth more than anything.

Now he was looking up the same way, but the sky above the parking lot was washed out by city lights. An orange glow from the streetlamps, haze from exhaust and smog. No stars visible anywhere.

Nothing to see. He lowered his head and looked straight at me through the windshield.

The expression on his face wasn't angry. Wasn't accusing. It was worse than that.

It was the look he used to give me when I'd promise to come to one of his basketball games and then cancel because I had to work late. Or when I'd tell him I'd visit for Thanksgiving and then stay at school instead.

That quiet disappointment. The kind that doesn't shout or blame. The kind that just accepts. Yeah. I knew you wouldn't come. He looked like he was waiting for me to get out of the car. To walk over to him. To finally show up.

And I wanted to. God, I wanted to. I wanted to open that door and run to him and tell him I was sorry. That I should have answered his calls. That I should have wired him the money. That I should have driven to Cleveland, found him, and brought him home.

That I should have been his sister.

But I couldn't move. Because if I opened that door, if I stepped out into the cold, he'd be gone. And I'd be standing alone in a parking lot, drunk, talking to air. Looking for stars that weren't there.

So I just sat there. Watching my little brother watch me. His face grew sadder. Not angry-sad. Just tired-sad.

The look of someone who'd been disappointed so many times they stopped being surprised by it. Then he turned and walked away into the dark between the buildings.

And I knew what he was walking toward. The same thing he'd walked toward that night eleven years ago when I didn't answer.

The alley on Fifth Street. The men waiting for him. The gun to his head.

"Leo, wait!" I grabbed the door handle.

But he was already gone. Just an empty parking lot. Just shadows and streetlights and the smell of exhaust.

I sat there with my hand on the door handle. Just me, alone in my car, with a bottle that was already half empty, even though I'd opened it only an hour earlier.

After that, Jack's Tavern became my office.

Wedged between a check-cashing joint and a discount cigarette store, it was the kind of bar where nobody asked what you did for work because the answer was obvious: nothing that mattered.

Mike, the bartender, looked like he'd seen every variety of wreckage walk through his doors. He didn't ask questions. He just poured doubles when you asked for them. A professional among the professionally ruined.

I used to stop there after Nordstrom shifts, just a drink or two before facing my apartment. Now it was my shift. My workplace. My whole world.

"Another vodka tonic?" Mike asked one Monday, not even glancing up.

"Make it a double."

It wasn't even 7 p.m. Happy hour for people who measured survival in shot glasses.

That's when he sat down next to me. Mid-forties, maybe. Stubble, tired eyes, the slouch of someone who'd been drinking since lunch. His voice had that loose, overconfident rhythm that comes when bad decisions start to sound good.

"You look too sophisticated for this place," he said, sliding onto the stool beside me like he owned it.

"Appearances can be deceiving." I lifted my glass, already on my third double.

He laughed like I'd cracked a joke instead of told the truth. "I like a woman with a sense of humor. Can I buy you another?"

The sober version of me would have said no. Would have known better. But she hadn't been around for months. Vodka had been making my decisions for a long time.

"Sure," I heard myself say.

His name was Dave. Or Dan. Or Derek. Something with a D that slid right out of my memory after he said it. He worked in construction or sales. Something about traffic, coffee from gas stations, long days in the city.

We talked about nothing. Baseball, the weather, how Chicago wasn't what it used to be. Just two strangers pretending to be normal people instead of what we were: broken, lonely, drinking on a Monday because there was nowhere else to go.

Three drinks turned into five. Five turned into a warm fog where the bar felt wrapped in cotton and his hand on my knee felt less like an intrusion and more like proof that I still existed.

"You want to continue this somewhere private?" he asked.

In any other life, I'd have laughed, stood up, and walked away. I didn't take men home from dive bars. I didn't let vodka and loneliness make my choices for me.

But this wasn't any other life. This was the life of someone who'd lost everything that mattered and was looking for anything, even for a night, to fill the empty space.

"Okay," I said.

I woke up in a place I didn't know. The walls were pale, with no pictures. Sunlight poured through bare windows, illuminating a living room that smelled like stale beer and old sadness. The kind of smell that sticks when someone lives alone too long.

I still had on yesterday's clothes, but not in the way I remembered putting them on. My shoes were near the door. My jacket was thrown over a chair. I could hear him. The man from the bar, Dave or Dan or Derek snoring in the bedroom.

I tried to piece the night together, but all I had were scraps: getting into his car, climbing some stairs, sitting on a couch that smelled like cigarettes. Then nothing. Blank tape.

My phone lit up with three missed calls from Linda and a text: *Sweetheart, I'm worried about you. Please call me back.*

My car keys were on a coffee table littered with empty bottles: beer, wine, even a cheap bottle of whiskey. I didn't remember drinking any of it, but the taste in my mouth said I had.

I walked six blocks to find my car. The morning air was sharp and bright. My head pounded with each step. People streamed past me on their way to jobs they hadn't been fired from, living lives they could remember, making choices they'd stand by when they sobered up. Normal people who didn't wake up in strangers' apartments wondering what they'd done.

Leo was waiting in the driver's seat when I finally got to my car.

He looked younger this time, like he'd stepped out of a memory from before everything fell apart. But his eyes were heavy with questions I couldn't answer and disappointments I couldn't fix.

His mouth moved, but no sound came out. I could read the shapes of the words anyway. *Is this who you want to be? Is this what my life was worth to you? Are you trying to follow me?*

"I don't remember what happened," I whispered.

He didn't answer. He just stared at me with those sad, knowing eyes that had been watching every wrong choice I'd made since he died. Then he lifted his hands. The same track marks as always. Purple, infected, burned into my brain from the morgue photos.

But this time, instead of pointing to my vodka bottle, he pointed to the stranger's apartment behind me.

I understood. Even without words, I understood. We were both trading pieces of ourselves for temporary relief from pain too big to hold. The only difference was the substance and the setting.

I started the car with shaking hands and drove home, his silent accusations echoing in the blank spaces where my memory should have been.

That night I sat on the air mattress in my studio apartment, surrounded by empty bottles, trying to figure out how I'd drifted so far from who I used to be.

But thinking was dangerous. Thinking led to questions about blackouts and strangers and whether I'd become the kind of person who put herself in situations she couldn't remember or control. So I opened another bottle and drank until the questions dulled.

My phone lit up again. Linda's name. For the twentieth time. I watched it ring. Watched her name glow in the dark. I couldn't make myself answer.

Because what would I say? That I was fine? That I had it under control?

The lies felt too heavy to carry anymore. The phone stopped ringing. It started again thirty seconds later. She wasn't going to stop. I knew that stubbornness. I had grown up with it.

My chest felt tight, as if my ribs were crushing my lungs.

I looked around the apartment. Empty bottles lined up on the counter. Furniture I couldn't afford to replace. Dishes I hadn't washed in a week. The air mattress I slept on because I'd sold my bed for rent money.

This was my life now.

Twenty-four years old. Master's degree from Ohio State. And I couldn't make it through a single day without blacking out.

The phone rang again. My hand shook as I reached for it. I hit the green button before I could talk myself out of it.

"Olivia." Not a question. Not relief. Just my name, flat and tired.

"Mom, I—"

"Are you drunk right now?"

The question hit like a slap.

"No." The lie came automatically.

"Don't." Her voice was sharp. Cold. "I can hear it in your voice. I've heard it every time you've called for the past six months."

Silence stretched between us. Heavy. Accusatory.

"I need help," I finally whispered.

"I know." She sounded exhausted. Done. "What do you want me to do about it?"

The words stung. I'd expected anger. Maybe disappointment. Not this bone-deep weariness.

"I don't know. I just... I can't do this anymore."

"Can't do what? Can't drink? Or can't deal with the consequences?"

My throat closed up. "Both."

She was quiet for a long time. I could hear her breathing. Controlled. Deliberate.

"You can come home," she said finally. "But I'm not going through this again. Not like with your father. Not like with Leo."

"I know."

"I mean it, Olivia. You come here, you get sober, or you leave. I'm done watching people I love destroy themselves."

Her voice cracked on the last word. Just a little. Enough to know she was still in there somewhere. Still cared. But barely.

"Okay," I said.

"When?"

"Tomorrow. I'll pack tonight."

"Drive carefully. Don't call me from the road unless it's an emergency."

Not "call me when you stop for gas." Not "call me if you need anything."

Just don't bother me unless you have to.

"Okay."

She hung up without saying goodbye.

I sat there in the dark with the phone in my hand. Shaking. Crying. More scared than relieved.

The pretending was over. I was going home. But Linda wasn't waiting with open arms. She was waiting with conditions. With exhaustion. With the kind of love that had been worn down to nothing but obligation.

I looked around at what was left of my life. The empty bottles. The air mattress. The ashes of everything good I'd had.

I stood up. The room spun a little. I started packing anyway because I had nowhere else to go and no one else to call. And because Linda said I could come home, even if she didn't want me there.

Tomorrow I'd drive to Ohio, but first I had to get through tonight without finishing the vodka. That felt impossible, but so did that phone call. And I'd done that.

Chapter Ten

Treatment or the Street

I CAME BACK TO Millfield with my life stuffed into garbage bags and the taste of shame heavy on my tongue.

Twenty-four years old. I'd clawed my way into Chicago, conquered McKinsey, learned to swirl wine like it was a language. And then I'd watched it all burn down on YouTube for strangers to laugh at.

Linda didn't hug me when I walked through the door. She just stepped aside, like she was letting a stranger into her house. Someone she recognized but didn't especially want to see.

"Leo's room is ready," she said.

Not *your old room*. Leo's room. As if to remind me whose space I was taking, whose life I'd failed to save.

The smell hit me the moment I stepped inside. Old cologne. Art supplies. That faint, chalky scent of paper and graphite from when he used to draw for the neighborhood kids. Before the drugs stole his steady hands and gentle heart.

I sat on his twin bed and stared at the crayon drawing still taped to his wall. Four stick figures under a yellow sun, "My Family" written in his seven-year-old handwriting. Back when he still believed we'd always be together.

His desk was exactly as he'd left it. Pencils in a chipped coffee mug. A half-finished sketch of what might have been a superhero. Scattered art supplies he'd been saving up to replace. The good drawing paper he'd bought with gas station paychecks back when he still had plans that stretched beyond the next high.

Everything was frozen in time, waiting for an artist who would never return to finish it.

That first week, I tried to be the daughter Linda remembered. I got up early. Made coffee. Scrolled job listings on my phone while the caffeine dulled the metallic taste of withdrawal. I applied for positions I knew I wouldn't get at companies that would Google my name and find the video before I even finished my interview.

Every call ended the same. Polite interest until they realized who I was and what I'd done. Then the shift in tone. *We'll be in touch.*

By noon, the sweating would start. By two, my heart would feel like it was trying to punch out of my chest. By four, I'd be at Giant Eagle, buying wine with trembling hands while the checkout girl pretended not to notice.

"Exactly like your father," a voice said from the empty passenger seat as I sat in the parking lot, drinking straight from the bottle. When I turned, no one was there. Just the echo of words I'd heard before.

"I'm nothing like him," I said to the empty car.

The silence felt like an answer.

Three weeks in, Linda found me passed out on the kitchen floor at seven a.m. An empty wine bottle was next to my head. Drool dried on my cheek. My body curled just like Dad's had the morning the paramedics carried him out.

She didn't yell. She didn't even cry. She just took a photo with her phone and left it on the counter next to my coffee cup. In the picture, I looked like a corpse that hadn't realized it was dead yet.

"We need to talk," Linda said when I finally staggered to the kitchen table, still in yesterday's clothes, still wearing the shame of waking up on linoleum.

"I'm fine. Just had a bad night."

"You've had nothing but bad nights since you moved home." She pulled out a manila folder thick with brochures. Treatment centers. Hazelden. Prices that made my empty bank account laugh. "I've been researching options."

"I don't need treatment, Mom. I just need to find work."

"With what references? You've been fired from every job you've had in the last six months."

Six months? I blinked. Time had stretched and shrunk like taffy, measured only by empty bottles and the cycle of withdrawal and relief.

"I can control this."

Linda laughed, sharp as broken glass. "That's what your father said. Right up until the doctor couldn't revive him."

The comparison hit like ice water, but I shoved it away. Dad had been different. Dad had been violent and mean. I was just... struggling. Managing grief with the tools I had.

"This is temporary," I said. "I just need to get back on my feet."

Linda opened the folder and spread the brochures across the table like she was dealing cards. Each one promised salvation for a price I couldn't afford and a surrender I wasn't ready to make.

"Look at these," she said, pointing to the glossy photos of serene campuses. "Thirty-day residential. Family therapy. Medical detox."

"I'm not like those people."

"What people?"

"Real addicts. People who've lost everything."

Linda's expression didn't change, but something flickered in her eyes. "What exactly do you think you haven't lost?"

The question hung in the air like smoke, and I couldn't answer it because the list of what I still had was getting shorter every day.

Linda stopped asking where I went during the day, stopped leaving meals in the fridge, and stopped pretending that anything she did might make a difference. We moved around each other like polite strangers, sharing a house but not a life, both of us waiting for something to break that would force a decision neither of us wanted to make.

The night I drove to the cemetery was Leo's birthday. What would have been his twenty-two. The age when normal kids celebrate with champagne, possibility, and futures they can't wait to live.

I brought a bottle of wine and sat next to his headstone in the dark. The grass was cold and wet against my legs, and the marble marker was smooth under my fingers like a worry stone.

"Happy birthday, Leo."

The wine tasted like regret, broken promises, and every conversation we'd never have.

Leo appeared beside his own grave, cross-legged in the grass like he was seven again and we were having a picnic in the backyard. But he wasn't looking at me; he was staring at his headstone like he was trying to read his own name and couldn't quite make it out.

"Do you remember what you promised me?" he asked without turning his head.

I remembered. The night before I left for Chicago, sitting in this same cemetery after Dad's funeral. I'd sworn I'd make something of myself, sworn I'd be successful enough to save everyone who needed saving.

"I tried," I whispered.

Leo finally looked at me, and his eyes were full of all the things that had never happened: college graduations, first apartments, wedding days, and all the birthdays we'd never celebrate together.

"Did you?"

The question cut deeper than any accusation could have.

I must have passed out there because the next thing I remember was bright flashlight beams and a police officer asking if I was all right.

"Ma'am, you can't sleep here. This is a cemetery."

"I'm visiting my brother."

"At 3 AM while intoxicated?"

The breathalyzer reading was .24. High enough to kill some people. High enough that the officer looked genuinely concerned for my survival instead of just annoyed by my behavior.

The Millfield jail smelled like disinfectant and desperation. I spent the night in a cell that reminded me of my studio apartment: small, gray, and hopeless, but with the added humiliation of having arrived there through my own choices.

Linda's expression when she picked me up the next morning told me everything I needed to know. This was the end of something. The last of her patience, perhaps. Or the last of her hope.

"Get in the car."

We drove home in silence. I pressed my face to the cool window and watched the town where I'd grown up slip past: the high school where I'd been valedictorian, the library where I'd studied every night, the gas station where Dad used to buy his whiskey when he thought nobody was watching.

All of it looked smaller now. Sadder. Like seeing childhood places through drunk eyes shrank them down to their real size, which had never been as big as memory made them.

"Uncle Mike is coming over tonight," Linda said as we pulled into the driveway. "We're having a meeting."

"About what?"

"About getting you help."

That evening, Uncle Mike spread brochures across the kitchen table like he was dealing cards in a game everyone loses: Hazelden, Betty Ford, places where famous people went to dry out before returning to their lives.

"She needs thirty days minimum," he told Linda as if I weren't sitting right there, my hands shaking so hard I couldn't hold my coffee cup steady. "Look at her."

I looked down at my hands, surprised by the tremor I hadn't noticed before. When had that started? When had my body begun betraying me in ways I couldn't hide?

"I don't need treatment," I said, though my voice sounded weak even to me. "I just need to cut back."

"Cut back from what?" Linda asked. Her voice was steady, but the tremor in her hands betrayed her. "A bottle of wine for breakfast? Two bottles for dinner? However much it takes to pass out in public places?"

"You were arrested at your brother's grave," Uncle Mike said, his voice gentle but unrelenting.

"She's not ready," Uncle Mike said quietly. "Look at her eyes. She's still fighting this."

"Then what do we do?" Linda asked.

"We set boundaries," he said. "Real ones. And we stick to them no matter how much it hurts."

He slid a business card across the table: Hazelden Betty Ford Center. A phone number printed in black ink that might as well have been a life preserver tossed to someone still convinced she knew how to swim.

"They have an opening Monday. I'll drive you myself if you want to go."

"What if I don't want to go?" My voice came out small.

Linda leaned forward. I saw something in her eyes I'd never seen before. Not disappointment, not anger, but terror. The kind of fear you get from watching the same film twice and already knowing how it ends.

"Then you find somewhere else to live."

"Mom, you can't kick me out. I'm your daughter."

"Your father was my husband for twenty-two years. That didn't stop me from leaving when his drinking became unmanageable." Her voice stayed steady even as her hands shook almost as badly as mine. "I went to Al-Anon after Leo died. I learned the difference between helping and enabling. I learned that love without boundaries isn't love at all."

"So what are my boundaries?"

"Treatment or the street."

Her words hit like a bucket of cold water, shocking me into a clarity I didn't want. This wasn't a negotiation. This wasn't another conversation I could charm or logic my way through. This was the end of the road, and I was the only one who could decide which way to turn.

Uncle Mike loaded my small suitcase into his car. The same bag I'd taken to college back when education felt like salvation and the future still looked like something worth reaching for.

"This is going to be hard," he said as we drove through the flat Ohio countryside toward Minneapolis. "But not as hard as dying."

"I'm not dying."

He glanced at me in the rearview mirror, his expression gentler than his words. "Honey, you're already dead. We're just trying to bring you back to life."

The intake nurse at Hazelden looked like she'd seen every kind of broken person walk through those doors. She asked about my drinking, my medical history, my family background, checking boxes on a form that would determine how much help I needed and how likely I was to survive it.

"Any family history of addiction?"

"My father drank. My brother used drugs. But I'm different from them."

She wrote something without looking up. "How are you different?"

I thought about it for a long moment. Same genes. Same trauma. Same solution for pain too big to hold.

"Actually, I'm not," I admitted. "I'm exactly the same."

My roommate was named Sharon. "Meth," she said during introductions. Four kids in foster care. Third time in treatment.

"What about you?" she asked that first night while I lay on the narrow bed trying not to think about how badly I wanted a drink.

"Wine."

"Fancy," she said. "I always wanted to be a wine drunk. Seemed more sophisticated than smoking crystal in gas station bathrooms."

I liked Sharon immediately. She had the kind of honesty that comes from having nothing left to lose and no energy left for pretending.

On day three, they put me in group therapy.Eight of us in a circle, chairs too close together, stories that all sounded like different versions of the same song. Different substances, different backdrops, but the same math: trading everything good for something that promised to make the pain stop.

"Who wants to share today?" Dr. Smith asked. He had the patience of someone who'd heard every excuse and the quiet wisdom to know which ones mattered.

Claire raised her hand. Mid-thirties, neat hair, nice clothes, the kind of woman who still looked like she had her life together until you noticed the tremor in her fingers.

"I keep telling myself I'm different from everyone else," she said. "That my drinking was more...reasonable. More justified."

Her eyes swept the circle and landed on me.

"I had a good job. A nice apartment. Expensive wine, not cheap beer. I drank at home, not in dive bars. I told myself that meant I was better than...well, than people like you."

The honesty hit me right in the chest.

"But yesterday my counselor asked me a question I can't stop thinking about. She said, 'If your drinking was so reasonable, why are you in treatment?' And I realized I didn't have an answer."

Her voice softened, but it cut deeper.

"Because reasonable people don't wake up in their own vomit wondering what happened to the last six hours. Reasonable people don't get fired from jobs they love for showing up drunk. Reasonable people don't choose alcohol over everything and everyone they care about."

She looked straight at me.

"And reasonable people don't end up in treatment centers, trying to learn how to live without the thing that's been slowly killing them for years."

The room went silent. I could hear my own heartbeat, feel eight pairs of eyes waiting to see if her story would crack something open in me.

It didn't crack me. It made me want to run. Because everything she said was true, and admitting that felt like dying.

"I don't belong here," I blurted. "My situation is different."

"How?" Dr. Smith asked.

"I'm not like her. I'm not like any of you. I have a college degree. I worked at McKinsey. I understand addiction from an analytical perspective."

Even as I said it, the words sounded hollow, but I couldn't stop.

"I can manage this on my own now that I understand the problem."

Sharon, my meth-addicted roommate with four kids in foster care, started laughing. Not mean laughter. Just the tired amusement of someone who's heard this speech before.

"Honey," she said, "every single person in this room has said those exact words. Different circumstances, same delusion."

"It's not a delusion," I said, though my voice was shaking.

"Then prove it," Sharon said. "Stay the thirty days. If you're so different, if you can manage this so easily, then treatment should be a breeze for someone as smart as you."

Her challenge hung in the air. She was right. If I was really in control, staying would be easy. But the idea of four more weeks here… listening, admitting, surrendering to the idea that I was powerless over something as simple as liquid in a bottle… felt like giving up everything I'd ever believed about myself.

"I've learned what I needed to learn," I said, standing up. "I understand my drinking patterns now. I can apply that knowledge on my own."

Dr. Smith didn't try to stop me. He just made a note on his clipboard. "The door is always open if you change your mind."

I signed myself out against medical advice that afternoon and called Uncle Mike to pick me up.

"That was fast," he said when I got in his car. His voice was careful, neutral.

"I learned what I needed to learn."

"Which was?"

"That I can manage this on my own. I understand the psychology now: the triggers, the patterns. I just need to apply cognitive behavioral techniques, and I'll be fine."

Uncle Mike nodded like he believed me, but his hands gripped the wheel tighter.

"Treatment works differently for different people," he said. "The important thing is that you're committed to getting better."

"I am," I said, and at that moment, I actually believed it.

Linda was waiting on the porch when we pulled up. She looked smaller, older, like the three days I'd been gone had aged her years.

"How was treatment?" she asked.

"Educational. I understand my drinking better now. I know what I need to do."

She nodded and went inside. She came back with my garbage bags.

"What's this?"

"Your things."

My stomach dropped like an elevator with cut cables. "I thought you said I could come home after treatment."

"I said you could come home after completing treatment. You left after three days."

"But I learned what I needed to learn! I understand the problem now!"

"Olivia." Her voice was gentle but final. "You've been telling me you understand the problem and can handle it for six months. Meanwhile, you've been arrested, fired from multiple jobs, and found unconscious in various places around town."

"This time is different."

"How?"

I opened my mouth to explain about cognitive behavioral techniques and triggers and all the things I'd learned about addiction psychology. But looking at her face... tired, heartbroken, absolutely done with my promises... I realized none of those words would matter.

She'd heard the same words from Dad for twenty years.

"Mom, please. I don't have anywhere else to go."

"I know." Her voice cracked slightly. "And I'm sorry about that. But I will not watch you drink yourself to death in my house. I won't be an accessory to your suicide."

She handed me a piece of paper with phone numbers written in her careful handwriting. "AA meetings. The crisis hotline. My number when you're ready to get serious about recovery."

"What if I die out there?"

"Then at least I won't have to watch it happen."

The words landed like a slap. But what hurt worse was the look in her eyes. This was killing her too, just in a different way.

Uncle Mike drove me to a motel on the edge of town without saying a word: the Millfield Motor Inn. Forty bucks a night, weekly rates posted on a plastic sign that flickered in the wind. The kind of place where dreams went to die and nobody asked why you were paying in cash.

"This doesn't have to be permanent," he said quietly as we pulled into the lot. "But it's what's available right now."

After he left, I sat on the thin mattress and took it all in: water stains on the ceiling shaped like countries on maps I'd never visit, carpet that smelled like cigarettes and despair, a graveyard of people who'd hit bottom hard enough to leave marks, a view of the parking lot where broken cars sat like abandoned hopes.

"Now what?" I asked the empty room.

I walked across the street to the gas station and spent my last twenty dollars on a bottle of wine. If this was rock bottom, I didn't want to feel it sober.

The first swallow tasted like surrender, like the end of every promise I'd ever made about being different from Dad, about being better than the circumstances that shaped me.

But it worked. For a few hours, the motel room stopped feeling like an ending and started to feel like just another place to exist until tomorrow forced decisions I wasn't ready to make.

For now, that had to be enough because it was all I had left.

Chapter Eleven

When Surviving Becomes Dying

T HE MOTEL MANAGER'S VOICE cut through my hang-over like fingernails on a chalkboard. "You're three days late on rent, Parker. And housekeeping says you've been drinking in the room."

I stood in his cramped office, swaying slightly, the air thick with old smoke and Pine-Sol that couldn't scrub out decades of other people's misery. Forty crumpled dollar bills trembled in my hands like dying butterflies.

"I have money," I rasped. "I can pay for one more night."

"Forty dollars doesn't cover what you owe, plus the carpet cleaning fee." He didn't even look up from the paperwork. "You've got an hour to clear out."

The door slammed behind me like a gunshot.

October air sliced through my thin jacket as I stood outside the motel with my two garbage bags. The manager had already locked the door behind me.

Forty dollars. That was it. That was everything I had left. I sat on the curb and tried to think. Tried to figure out what came next.

Forty dollars wouldn't get me another motel room. Not even the cheap ones. Not even for one night.

My phone was in my pocket. Dead. I'd stopped paying the bill two weeks ago. There was a payphone at the gas station across the street. I could see it from where I sat. One of the last ones left in the city.

I dug through my pockets and found three quarters. I crossed the street on shaky legs, picked up the receiver, and dialed the number I knew by heart. The one I'd promised myself I'd never call again.

Linda answered on the fourth ring. "Hello?"

"Mom, it's me."

Silence. Then a long exhale. "Olivia."

Not a greeting. Just my name. Flat. Tired.

"I got kicked out of my motel. I don't have anywhere to go."

"Where are you?"

"Cleveland. Route 90."

"How much have you been drinking?"

My hands were shaking. Had been shaking since I woke up. "I haven't had anything today."

"Don't lie to me."

"I'm not lying. I don't have money for alcohol. I don't have money for anything."

She was quiet for a long time. I could hear her breathing. Controlled. Deliberate.

"There's a detox center in Cleveland. Rosewood Recovery. They take people without insurance."

"Mom, please. I just need a place to stay. Just for tonight."

"And then what? Tomorrow you'll need another night. Next week you'll need money. Next month you'll need bail. I can't do this anymore, Olivia."

"I'm not asking you to—"

"Yes, you are. You're always asking. And I'm always giving. And nothing ever changes."

My throat tightened. "Please."

"Call me when you're ready to get help. Real help. Not just a place to crash until the next disaster."

The line went dead.

I stood there with the receiver in my hand, the dial tone buzzing in my ear. She'd hung up on me. My own mother had hung up on me. I put the receiver back and stared at the quarters in my hand.

The homeless shelter was six blocks away. I could walk.

The shelter was a big brick building with bars on the windows. People sat on the steps smoking. Some looked worse than I did. Some looked better. All of them looked tired.

Inside smelled like bleach and sweat.

"You need intake?" A woman at the desk didn't look up from her clipboard.

"Yes. I need a bed for tonight."

"We're full. Have been for three weeks."

"Please. It's supposed to go down to thirty degrees tonight. I'll sleep on the floor. Anywhere."

She finally looked at me, taking in the garbage bags, the shaking hands, the desperation.

"We do intake every morning at 8 AM. If you're here and we have space, we'll take you. But right now we're at capacity."

"Where am I supposed to sleep tonight?"

"There's a warming center on Delmar. It opens at 10 PM. First come, first served."

She handed me a flyer. My hands shook too much to take it.

"The warming center has a no-alcohol policy," she added. "You'll have to pass a breathalyzer to get in."

I walked out without the flyer.

The church on Seventh Street was twelve blocks away. St. Mary's. The one with the soup kitchen. My legs hurt by the time I got there. My stomach was empty. It had been empty since yesterday.

The doors were locked. A sign taped to the glass read: "Due to budget cuts, soup kitchen now operates Wednesdays and Saturdays only."

Today was Thursday.

I sat on the church steps and put my head in my hands. Forty dollars. Not enough for a motel. Not enough for anything that mattered.

The warming center would be open in four hours. But I'd have to stay sober. I had to sit there shaking while the withdrawals made me want to claw my skin off. I had to face the questions, the pity, and the rules.

I couldn't do it. I couldn't make it four more hours without something to stop the shaking. Something to quiet the burning in my chest.

I stood up and picked up my garbage bags.

The gas station across from the motel was a mile back. They sold vodka. Cheap vodka. The kind that burned going down but made everything stop hurting. I started walking back toward the gas station.

Each step felt like defeat. Like proof that Linda was right. That I'd never change. That I was exactly what everyone thought I was. But I couldn't stop shaking. I couldn't think straight. I couldn't face another night sober, cold, and alone.

By the time I reached the gas station, the sun was setting. The temperature was dropping.

I sat on the curb with my garbage bags. Forty dollars in my pocket. No phone. No family. No options left.

Just the gas station behind me selling vodka. And after that? After that, I'd figure something out. I always did. Even if "figuring it out" meant doing things I'd promised myself I'd never do. Even if it meant becoming someone I didn't recognize.

I just had to make it through tonight.

A truck driver honked as he pulled in. Big rig, Arizona plates, the kind of long-haul guy who'd been on the road for days. He parked and glanced at me sitting on the curb.

"You okay, honey?" he asked. Kind eyes, graying hair. Probably somebody's father heading home after weeks away.

"Fine," I said, but my voice cracked.

He looked at my face, my bags, the bottle I wasn't hiding well. "You need a ride somewhere?"

I looked at him. Really looked. Wedding ring. Concern written all over him. A decent man who probably just wanted to help. But decent men didn't want what I was about to offer.

"I need money," I blurted. "Twenty dollars."

His expression changed. Sad, not disgusted. Like he'd seen this before, maybe had daughters of his own.

"For what?"

I couldn't say it. I couldn't form the words that would make it real. I just stared at him until understanding dawned.

"Ah, sweetheart." He shook his head. "You don't want to do that."

"I don't want to do anything," I said. "But I need money and you need... something. It's just business."

He was quiet for a long moment, studying me like a puzzle he didn't want to solve. Then he pulled out his wallet and handed me a twenty.

"Here. But not for that. Just because you need it."

I stared at the bill. "What's the catch?"

"No catch. Sometimes people just need help."

My fingers shook as I took it. "Thank you."

"Get somewhere safe tonight," he said. "You're somebody's daughter. Somebody who loves you."

He walked inside, leaving me on the curb with sixty dollars and the crushing knowledge that even strangers could see how far I'd fallen.

But sixty dollars wasn't enough. Not for a room, not for food, not for the amount of alcohol I needed to get through another night without unraveling completely.

I finished the vodka and walked to the truck stop on the edge of town. The lot was full of big rigs and cars that had seen better decades. Women drifted between trucks like ghosts, some so thin they looked like they might blow away.

I stood by the entrance, stomach cramping with hunger and withdrawal, hands shaking so badly I could barely hold the empty bottle.

A man in his fifties climbed down from a red truck. Overweight, baseball cap. The kind of guy who probably had a wife somewhere but had been on the road too long.

"You working?" he asked, not unkindly.

The word caught in my throat like broken glass. Working. Like this was a job instead of the annihilation of everything I used to be.

"Twenty dollars," I whispered.

He nodded toward his truck. "Cab's got a sleeper. Five minutes."

I followed on legs that felt like water. The cab smelled like diesel, air freshener, and loneliness. The mattress in the sleeper looked like it hadn't been washed in months.

"You don't look like you've been doing this long," he said, still not moving toward me.

"I haven't."

"You sure you want to?"

I thought about the forty dollars in my pocket. About the burn in my chest that only vodka could quiet. About sleeping on the street in October without money for shelter.

"I'm sure."

What happened next took five minutes but felt like five hours. I stared at the ceiling and tried to leave my body, to pretend this was happening to some other woman. Someone who'd made different choices.

When it was over, he handed me twenty dollars without meeting my eyes.

"You should get off the streets," he said softly. "This ain't no life for a girl like you."

A girl like me. Like he could still see traces of who I used to be beneath the desperation and the alcohol.

I stumbled out of the truck and into the bathroom, my knees hitting the tile as my stomach expelled everything inside it. Bile burned the back of my throat until there was nothing left to come up but air. I splashed cold water on my face and raised my head toward the cracked mirror.

The woman looking back at me wasn't me. Hollow cheeks. Dead eyes. Skin the color of old newsprint. This was the version of myself I used to imagine I'd never become. This was bottom.

I walked back across the lot on shaky legs and found another truck. Then another. By midnight I had enough crumpled cash for a room and more vodka. Enough to hold off the shakes for another day. Enough to hate myself with a kind of purity that felt like drowning in poison.

The next night I was back at the truck stop. The routine had set in with terrifying speed: stand in the shadows; wait for someone to approach; negotiate; disappear for a few minutes; collect cash. Repeat.

I told myself I was surviving. I told myself it was temporary. I told myself I'd stop as soon as I figured out something else. But "something else" never came. Surviving started to feel less like living and more like dying in slow motion.

That's when the man in khakis came toward me.

"You look like you could use some assistance," he said. His voice was smooth, almost too smooth, like he was reading lines from a book.

I turned and looked at him. Everything about him was too neat for a truck stop at night. His pants had sharp creases, like they had just been ironed. His shirt was bright white, without a wrinkle in sight. His hair was combed into place like it had been done with a ruler. Even his shoes were shiny.

He didn't belong there. Neither did I, once.

"I'm fine," I said, even though we both knew I wasn't.

"Are you?" He sat down on the concrete barrier beside me without asking. His cologne was heavy, expensive, not like the cheap aftershave the truckers wore. "You seem to be experiencing some unfortunate circumstances."

His words didn't sound right. Too formal. Like he'd learned to talk from a training video instead of real life.

"I have a residence nearby," he said. "Clean accommodations, hot shower, proper nourishment." His smile stretched across his face like something he had rehearsed in front of a mirror. "Sometimes we all require assistance from strangers during difficult times."

I should have said no. I should have listened to the warning in my gut. But I was tired. So tired of truck cabs and gas station bathrooms. Tired of wiping my face with paper towels, tired of pretending I was still human.

"What do you want?" I asked.

"Perhaps some companionship," he said. "I find myself experiencing considerable loneliness in the evenings." He stood up, brushing at his already perfect shirt. "I would compensate you generously for your time and company."

"How generously?"

"Two hundred dollars. For the entire evening."

Two hundred. More than I had made in a week. Enough for food. Enough for a better place to sleep. Enough vodka to last me days.

"Okay," I said. My body was screaming at me to run, but my mouth agreed anyway.

The ride took about fifteen minutes. The neighborhoods kept getting nicer the farther we drove. Big old houses with trees lining the streets. Coffee shops with charming signs. Restaurants with tables outside and people laughing over glasses of wine.

The kind of places I used to go with Raymond. The kind of life I used to pretend was mine.

He parked in a garage attached to a tall building made of glass and steel. There was a doorman in the lobby and cameras everywhere. Places like this didn't usually let women like me walk inside.

"I'm on the fourteenth floor," he said in that same businesslike tone. "The building has excellent security protocols and privacy measures."

The elevator doors opened right into his apartment.

A penthouse. My breath caught in my throat.

Windows stretched from floor to ceiling, revealing the city lights spread out below. Hardwood floors that probably cost more than I'd made in a year. White couches, glass tables, modern paintings that looked like they had price tags bigger than my former rent. Everything was spotless. Too spotless. Like no one actually lived there.

The air even smelled artificial, like pine and something chemical, pumped in on purpose.

"Your apartment is…" I didn't know how to finish the sentence.

"Yes," he said. "I've invested considerable resources in establishing appropriate accommodations. My family is successful. They manage a large media corporation. I work in their business development division. It's stressful work, which is why I require companionship."

He took two glasses from the cabinet, moving with the same stiff precision as before, and poured wine from a French bottle sitting on the counter. Wine that probably cost more than my motel rent for a week.

"Please, have a seat." He pointed toward the white couch. "We should get acquainted over wine. I prefer to establish rapport before proceeding to more intimate activities. It is more civilized."

I lowered myself onto the couch, afraid I might stain it. The cushions were so soft it felt like sinking into clouds.

He handed me a glass and sat in a chair across from me, treating it like a meeting instead of what it really was.

"So tell me about yourself," he said. "Your background. Your circumstances. I find personal narratives quite fascinating."

I drank the wine in a long swallow. It was smooth, rich. The kind I used to pretend to know about at McKinsey dinners.

"I was a consultant," I said. "McKinsey. Got fired. Everything fell apart after that."

"McKinsey. Quite impressive." He sipped delicately. "My mother would be intrigued. She respects strategic thinkers. Of course, your current circumstances suggest some poor decisions."

The words felt clinical, like he was reviewing a report.

"Yeah. Poor decisions." I drank more. The warmth spreading in my chest was the only thing making the strangeness of it all bearable.

"Life often presents suboptimal outcomes," he said. "The key is adapting with appropriate strategies." He stood. "Would you like more wine? I have an excellent collection. My family has connections with vineyards in Napa Valley."

"Sure."

He poured more wine into my glass and some for himself as well. He sat back in his chair with that same careful distance, like a teacher at a desk.

"My parents have high expectations," he said, swirling his glass as if he were on TV. "Metrics for success that can be hard to meet. Sometimes the pressure calls for certain stress-relief activities. I'm sure you understand."

I didn't. I didn't understand why someone with a penthouse, family money, and a job at his mother's company had to pick up women like me from truck stops.

But I drank the wine and nodded anyway. Two hundred dollars was two hundred dollars. Understanding wasn't part of the deal.

He kept talking for another half hour. Corporate words about his job, his family, and the "disruption cycles" in media. I let his voice wash over me like static on a broken radio. I drank and tried not to listen.

Halfway through my third glass, the edges of the room began to blur. My tongue felt heavy. My arms felt far away. The lights doubled, then smeared.

"Did you put something in my drink?" My voice came out wrong. Slurred.

The polite smile dropped off his face.

"Yes." Simple. Matter-of-fact. Like I'd asked if he'd locked the door.

I tried to stand, but my legs wouldn't work. The room tilted sideways.

"I need to leave." The words came out thick and slow.

"You're not leaving." He wasn't smiling anymore. Just watching me with cold, empty eyes. "Sit down before you fall."

My legs gave out. I collapsed back onto the couch.

He stood up and walked to the kitchen. I heard a drawer open and close. He came back with something in his hands. Silk scarves. Expensive ones. Dark red.

"What are you—"

"Don't scream." His voice was calm. Flat. "The walls are thick, but I'd rather not test them."

He grabbed my wrist. I tried to pull away, but my arm felt like it weighed a thousand pounds. He tied the scarf around it. Tight. Then pulled my arm up and secured it to something behind the couch.

"Stop." I tried to fight. Tried to move. Nothing worked right.

He didn't answer. He just tied my other wrist and then moved to my ankles.

I was trapped, tied to his furniture like an animal.

He stepped back, looked at me, and adjusted one of the scarves like he were straightening a picture frame.

"That's better."

My heart was hammering. I could feel it, but I couldn't feel my hands anymore.

"Why are you doing this?"

He looked at me like I'd asked a stupid question. "Because I want to."

That was it. No explanation. No justification. Just because he wanted to.

He walked away. I heard him in another room, water running, humming something under his breath.

When he came back, he'd changed. No more khakis and a white shirt. Now just sweatpants. Nothing else.

"Please." My voice cracked. "Please don't."

"You came here willingly." He said it like he was correcting me on a fact. "You walked into my apartment. You drank the wine I gave you. You made this very easy."

"I didn't know—"

"Of course you didn't know. That's the point." He knelt in front of me, his face inches from mine. "You thought I was safe. Clean clothes. Nice apartment. Polite manners."

He touched my face. I tried to jerk away, but the scarves held me still.

"You're not the first girl who thought that." His voice was soft now. Almost gentle. Worse than if he'd been yelling. "You won't be the last."

Tears ran down my face. I couldn't stop them.

He stood up and started untying my ankles from the couch. "We're going to the bedroom now. Don't fight. The drug makes you clumsy, and I don't want you getting hurt."

Getting hurt. Like he cared. Like he wasn't about to—

He lifted me. My body was dead weight. He carried me like I was nothing. Down a hallway, through a door.

The bedroom was dark, with no windows. The walls were a deep burgundy color that looked black in the dim light.

He put me on the bed and started retying the scarves to the bedposts. My wrists. My ankles. Spread out. Helpless.

"There we go." He stepped back, looked at his work, satisfied.

Classical music started playing. Violins. Coming from speakers I couldn't see.

"I like Bach for this," he said, not to me, just saying it out loud. "Mother always played Bach when she was working. Said it helped her focus."

He moved around the room. I could hear him but couldn't turn my head to see. The drug had me now. Everything felt heavy and distant.

His hand on my shoulder. Then my arm. Clinical. Like a doctor conducting an exam.

"You're probably wondering if anyone will come looking for you." His voice was matter-of-fact. Conversational. "They won't. Girls like you disappear all the time, and nobody notices."

I tried to speak. Nothing came out.

"That's why I chose you." He said it simply. Honestly. "No family who cares. No real home. No job that'll miss you. You're nobody's priority."

The truth of it hit harder than anything physical could.

"Perfect," he said softly.

The music got louder. The violins building to something. Then, his hands were on me again. And I couldn't fight. Couldn't scream. Couldn't do anything but lie there while my mind screamed and my body refused to listen.

The last thing I remembered clearly was the music. Those violins. And his voice, distant now, saying something about efficiency.

Then everything went black.

I woke up on the cold floor of his perfect apartment.

The hardwood stung my cheek. My clothes were ripped. Time was gone, hours torn away like pages from a book.

Everything hurt. My throat was raw. My ribs throbbed. Purple fingerprints wrapped my neck like a necklace I never wanted.

Morning light poured through the floor-to-ceiling windows. I'd lost an entire night.

I pushed myself upright. My arms shook. The apartment was empty. He was gone. Left me there like trash on a polished floor.

Two hundred dollars lay on the coffee table. Neat, crisp bills. Payment for services rendered. I grabbed the money with shaking hands and stumbled to the elevator. Pressed the button. Prayed no one would see me like this.

The elevator moved so slowly. Each floor felt like an eternity of shame.

The doorman looked at me as I passed. His eyes took in the bruises, the torn clothes, my unsteady steps. He didn't say a word. Didn't ask if I needed help. Just watched me leave like I was something dirty he didn't want to touch.

I made it to the bus stop and sat on the bench. Every part of me ached. But the worst pain wasn't my body; it was knowing that somewhere he was probably getting ready for work, showering in his marble bathroom, putting on another pressed shirt, and walking into his mother's company like nothing had happened.

Like I didn't matter. Like what he did was just another transaction in a world that valued some people and discarded others.

The bus came. I got on and rode toward the emergency room because I couldn't think of anywhere else to go.

Chapter Twelve

Hope in the Hospital

When I walked into the emergency room, the lights were so bright they felt like knives, stabbing straight through my skull. My throat was raw, like I'd been screaming for hours. Purple fingerprints ringed my neck like a necklace I hadn't agreed to wear. The smell of antiseptic floated under the taste of fear that still coated my tongue.

"Can you tell me your name?" the nurse asked. She had kind eyes and hands that smelled faintly of soap and lavender lotion.

"Olivia Parker."

"What happened to you, Olivia?"

I told her about the man. About his apartment that smelled like death dressed up as pine air freshener. About waking up on his floor with my clothes torn and hours missing from my memory like pages ripped out of a book.

She wrote it all down slowly, making soft noises meant to sound comforting. Then the doctor came in with tired eyes and a clipboard.

"We ran some tests," he said, not quite meeting my gaze. "Your blood alcohol level is .18. That's a level that would make most people unconscious."

"He drugged me."

"The only substance in your system is alcohol. A significant amount."

"I'd been drinking before, but not enough to black out completely. He put something in the wine."

The doctor exchanged a look with the nurse. The kind of look that said they'd heard this story before from girls like me.

"Miss Parker, given your... situation... and your blood alcohol level, it's more likely you drank too much and don't remember consenting to rough sex."

Situation. Like prostitution was a lifestyle choice instead of rock bottom with a price tag.

The rape kit was humiliating in ways I didn't know were possible. Evidence collection. Photographs. Questions about details that floated just out of reach like shards of broken glass.

The police who came in were mismatched. The older one looked like he'd been doing this job since before I was born. Thick neck, wedding ring worn thin, eyes that had seen too much to be surprised by anything. The younger one couldn't have been more than twenty-five. Clean-shaven face. New shoes. The kind of nervous energy that came from wanting to do this job right and not yet knowing how.

"I'm Detective Johnson," the older one said, settling into the plastic chair like it was his personal throne. "This is Officer Anderson. We need to ask you some questions about what happened tonight."

Officer Anderson pulled out his notepad, but his hands hesitated over the blank page like he wasn't sure where to start.

"You had been drinking," Johnson said. Not a question. A statement.

"Yes, but—"

"And you were engaging in prostitution."

"I was trying to survive."

Johnson wrote something down. His face didn't change at all. "And you went to his apartment voluntarily."

"Yes, but he—"

"And you can't remember what happened during the encounter."

"Because he drugged me."

Johnson looked up then. His expression was the same one I'd seen on the doctor's face. The same one I'd been getting since the moment I walked through the ER doors.

Like he'd already decided what kind of girl I was and what kind of story I was telling.

"Look," he said, not unkindly, but not kindly either. "We'll process the evidence, send it to the lab, and file a report. But I'm going to be straight with you. These cases are tough."

"What does that mean?"

Officer Anderson glanced at his partner, then back at me. "It means we're going to investigate, get your toxicology results, and see if we can identify the guy from the description you gave."

"But?"

"But a jury looks at the circumstances—" Johnson started.

"The circumstances don't matter," Anderson interrupted. His voice was quiet but firm. "If someone assaulted you, that's a crime, regardless of the circumstances."

Johnson shot him a look. Not angry, exactly. More like a teacher watching a student who hasn't learned the lesson yet.

"In theory, you're right," Johnson said. "In practice? Defense attorneys are going to tear this apart. A prostitute who was drinking, who went to his apartment voluntarily, who can't remember what happened—" He shook his head. "That's not a winnable case. The DA won't touch it."

"So he gets away with it?" My voice came out smaller than I wanted.

Johnson sighed. It was the sound of a man who'd had this conversation too many times. "I'm not saying he should. I'm saying he probably will. These guys know how to pick their victims. They know who's not going to be believed."

The words hit like a slap. Not because they were cruel, but because they were true.

Officer Anderson was still writing, his pen moving fast across the paper like he was trying to capture every word I'd said. When he looked up, his expression was different from his partner's. Not pity, exactly. More like anger on my behalf.

"We're going to try," he said. "We'll run the DNA from the kit, check for priors, talk to his neighbors, see if anyone saw or heard anything." He pulled a card from his pocket and set it on the hospital tray beside me. "This is the number for the Sexual Assault Crisis Center. They have advocates who can help you navigate the system, answer questions, and go with you to court if it gets that far."

"If," Johnson corrected. "Not when."

Anderson ignored him. "And this—" He pulled out another card. "This is my direct number. If you remember anything else, if he contacts you, if you need anything." He met my eyes. "I mean it. Anything."

For a second, I saw something in his face that I hadn't seen in weeks. Someone who looked at me and saw a person instead of a problem. Someone who believed me even when the evidence said he shouldn't.

"Thank you," I whispered.

Johnson stood, tucking his notepad into his jacket. "We'll be in touch when the lab results come back. Could be a few weeks. Maybe longer."

Anderson stood too, but slower. Like he didn't want to leave yet. Like there was something else he wanted to say but didn't know how.

"I'm sorry this happened to you," he said finally. The words were simple, but they landed with weight. "And I'm sorry the system makes it so hard to get justice."

Johnson was already at the door. "Anderson. Let's go."

Officer Anderson nodded at me one more time, then followed his partner out.

I sat there alone with the two business cards on my tray.

The discharge papers came an hour later. Instructions about follow-up care I wouldn't follow, pamphlets about resources I wouldn't use, a prescription for antibiotics I couldn't afford to fill.

"You're free to go," the nurse said. The same kind-eyed woman from earlier. But her kindness felt hollow now. Useless.

I picked up the cards Officer Anderson had left: crisis center, his direct number. I looked at them for a long time. Then, I put them in my pocket and walked out.

The hospital doors opened onto November air that felt like breathing broken glass. Every step made my ribs ache. My throat burned when I swallowed. But the worst pain was knowing he was out there somewhere, free, maybe already hunting for his next victim.

The bus stop bench was cold and hard. I sat there watching normal people move through their normal lives: a woman pushing a stroller, an old man walking his dog, college kids laughing about some joke I'd never get.

All of them lived in a world where they mattered, where if something bad happened to them, someone would fight for justice, where they had homes to go to and people who'd notice if they disappeared.

I wasn't part of that world anymore. Maybe I never had been.

The bottle of vodka hidden in my jacket felt heavier than it should. Last twenty dollars spent on the only medicine that still worked. I twisted the cap off and drank straight from the bottle, not caring who saw.

The alcohol burned going down but dulled the pain, made the rage simmer instead of boil over, made it feel like maybe I could make it through one more day.

But as I sat there drinking, I started counting: how many more days like this, how many more nights of selling myself to strangers, how many more times I'd wake up somewhere I didn't remember with bruises I couldn't explain, how many more police officers would look at me with pity they couldn't turn into help.

The vodka went down easier after the first few sips. It always did. My body was grateful for the numbness even while my brain knew it was poison.

By the time the bottle was half empty, I'd made a decision.

I couldn't do this anymore. I couldn't survive another day of being less than human. I couldn't handle another night in a truck cab or a sterile apartment with a man who saw me as disposable.

Officer Anderson had tried to be kind, had given me his card, had said "anything."

But what could he do? What could anyone do?

The system had already decided I didn't matter: the doctor, the prosecutor who wouldn't take my case, the defense lawyers who'd tear me apart, the jury who'd look at me and see trash.

I'd tried everything. Tried legitimate work. Tried getting sober. Tried asking for help. Tried fighting back. Nothing had worked. I just kept falling further down until there wasn't any bottom left to hit.

Leo had found a way out. Dad had found a way out. Maybe it was time I stopped pretending I'd never follow them.

I pulled Officer Anderson's card out of my pocket. I looked at the number one more time. Then, I put it back. And I stood up. I started walking toward the Millfield River.

The bridge over the Millfield River was a ten-minute walk from the bus stop. I'd driven over it thousands of times growing up, never once thinking about how far the drop was or how cold the water would be in November.

The bridge was higher than it looked from the road. Up close, the water moved fast, black as oil under the November sky. If I jumped, no one would find me for days. Maybe weeks. Long enough for it to be over before anyone dragged me back to another hospital and told me to keep living.

The metal railing burned my palms. I gripped it and swung one leg over, then the other, until I was sitting on the edge with my feet dangling into empty air. This was how my story would end. Not with a dramatic rescue. Not with some revelation about how life was still worth living. Just a drunk, broken woman too tired to keep existing.

"You sure about this, princess?"

I almost slipped. Dad was sitting next to me on the railing, looking exactly as he had the day before he died. Yellow skin, hollow cheeks, but his eyes were clear. Clearer than they'd been in years.

"I can't do this anymore," I whispered. "I can't keep living like this."

"Like what?"

"Like nothing. Like garbage. Like someone who doesn't matter."

He let the silence stretch. His feet swung over the water too. "I used to think about this bridge," he said finally. "Especially toward the end, when the drinking stopped working and I could feel everything falling apart."

"Why didn't you?"

"Because I was a coward. Jumping would've been honest about what I was doing to myself, and I wasn't ready to be honest yet." He turned his head toward me. "Are you ready to be honest?"

"About what?"

"About why you're really here."

I stared down at the river. It looked peaceful, quiet. "Because I can't take the pain anymore."

"What pain?"

"All of it. Leo. You. What happened last night. What I've become."

"And you think dying will make that better?"

I tried to laugh, but it came out like a sob. "I think dying will make it stop."

"Will it though?" Dad's voice softened. "Or will it just hand that pain to somebody else?"

"Who? There's nobody left who cares if I live or die."

"You sure about that?"

Before I could answer, Leo appeared on my other side. Not the hollow-eyed ghost I'd been seeing for months, but Leo at fifteen. Messy hair, crooked grin, the brother who used to make me laugh no matter how bad things got.

"Remember sneaking out to watch the sunrise?" he asked. "That summer before everything went to hell?"

I remembered. Dad was drinking but still functional. Mom was working double shifts. Leo and I would climb out the window at five a.m. and walk to the river to watch the sun come up over the water.

"We'd sit right here on this bridge," he said. "And you'd tell me all your plans. College. Career. The perfect life you were going to build."

"That was before I knew how everything would turn out."

"Was it?" Leo tilted his head. "Or did you already know life would try to break you, and you decided to fight anyway?"

The vodka made me dizzy. Or maybe it was the height. Or maybe it was just sitting on a bridge railing talking to dead people like it was normal.

"I'm tired of fighting," I said.

"I know," Leo said. "I was tired too. That's why I chose the pills instead of keeping going. And you know what I learned?"

"What?"

"Dying doesn't solve anything. It just ends the story before you find out how it could have changed."

I looked at him. Really looked. He seemed so solid I almost reached out to grab his hand, drag him back with me.

"What if it doesn't change?" I asked. "What if this is all there is?"

"Then at least you'd know," Dad said. "Instead of guessing."

I sat there on the railing, drunk and broken and talking to ghosts, trying to picture waking up tomorrow. Another day of surviving instead of living. Another job, another cheap room, another way to keep going when everything inside me was screaming to stop. It felt impossible. But so did jumping.

"I don't know how," I whispered.

"How to what?" Leo asked.

"How to keep going."

"One day at a time," Dad said. "Same way you've made it this far."

I closed my eyes and felt the November wind cut through my jacket. Smelled the river, the dead leaves, my own fear. Heard traffic behind me, water below me, my heart beating too fast. When I opened my eyes, they were gone. Just me, sitting on a bridge, drunk and desperate and still breathing.

I climbed back over the railing onto solid ground. My legs shook so hard I had to sit on the sidewalk before I could walk. The walk back to the bus stop felt like the longest journey of my life.

Six weeks later, I was still alive. Barely. But alive.

I had a room in a boarding house that rented by the week. Forty dollars for a thin mattress on the floor and a bathroom at the end of the hall that smelled like mildew and bleach. The walls were stained, and the carpet was sticky, but the door locked. That counted for something.

I'd stopped going to the truck stop. Stopped selling myself. Not because I'd found dignity. Not because of self-respect. Just because every time I thought about it, I threw up.

When I left the hospital, they had given me a small card. "Check back in six weeks," the nurse had said, "to make sure everything's healing properly." I'd thrown the card in a trash can.

But six weeks passed. I was still having nightmares about his hands on my neck. Still seeing his empty doll eyes every time I closed mine. Still waking up in the dark, gasping, clawing at my throat to make sure I was alone.

So I went back. The clinic wasn't the emergency room. It was smaller, quieter. Beige walls, soft voices. People waiting for normal checkups, not crises.

A nurse called my name. "Olivia Parker?"

I followed her to an exam room that smelled like antiseptic and latex gloves. She wrapped a cuff around my arm, asked routine questions, and typed on her computer. "The doctor will be right in," she said, smiling politely but not warmly.

Dr. Smith came in a few minutes later. Older. Wire-rimmed glasses. Eyes that looked at me instead of through me. She read my chart, asked about my nightmares, and examined the bruises on my throat that were now faint yellow shadows.

"Everything appears to be healing well," she said. "The bruising should be gone in a week or two."

"Good," I said, already reaching for my jacket, thinking about the bottle of vodka waiting in my room.

"However," Dr. Smith said, looking at her screen, "we ran routine bloodwork as part of your follow-up. There's something we need to discuss."

My stomach dropped. "What kind of something?"

"Your pregnancy test came back positive."

The room tilted. I gripped the edge of the table.

"That's not possible."

"I'm afraid it is. Based on your hormone levels, you're approximately six weeks along."

Six weeks.

The same six weeks since that night. Since the penthouse. Since the drugged wine. Since the dark room with the Bach playing and his hands on me while I couldn't move.

"No," I whispered. "No, no, no."

"I understand this is difficult news, especially given the circumstances of your assault—"

"It's his." The words came out flat. Dead. "The baby is his. The rapist's."

Dr. Smith set her tablet down and rolled her chair closer. "You have options, Olivia. This is your choice to make. We have counselors who can help you understand—"

"I need to think," I said, standing up too fast. The room spun.

"Please wait. Let me give you some information about prenatal care, about the resources available—"

But I was already in the hallway, pushing out the door into cold March air that sliced my face and chest.

Pregnant. With the baby of a man who drugged me and tied me down and played classical music while he—

I made it to a trash can and vomited.

I walked for an hour after leaving the clinic. Didn't know where I was going. Just walking because standing still felt like drowning.

Six weeks pregnant.

The words kept repeating in my head. Six weeks. A heart beating. Arms and legs starting to form. All of it growing while I'd been trying to die.

The liquor store on Maple Street was still open. I stood outside staring at the neon sign. The word "OPEN" flickered. On and off. On and off.

I went in. Twelve dollars for the cheapest vodka. I had fourteen in my pocket. The cashier didn't look at my face. Just took my money and put the bottle in a paper bag.

I sat on the curb outside. Opened it. The smell hit me first. Sharp and familiar.

Six weeks. That's what the doctor said. Six weeks of poisoning something that was trying to live.

I drank anyway. It burned going down. Like always. But it didn't make anything better. Didn't quiet the screaming in my head.

I thought about the man in khakis. His empty eyes. His hands on me while I couldn't move.

This baby was half him. Half monster. I drank more.

By the time the bottle was half empty, the sun had set. The temperature dropped. I was shaking, but I didn't know if it was from cold or something else.

I walked back to the boarding house. My room was dark. The mattress on the floor looked like a grave.

I finished the bottle. Let the vodka pull me under until everything went black.

I woke up on the floor. Sunlight coming through the dirty window. My head pounding like someone was splitting it open with an axe.

The empty bottle was next to me. The pregnancy pamphlets were scattered everywhere. I picked one up. Read it with eyes that barely focused.

"Fetal Alcohol Syndrome. Developmental delays. Physical abnormalities."

I'd done that. Every drink for six weeks. Poisoning it. My stomach turned. I ran to the bathroom and threw up. Nothing but bile. My throat burned.

A woman at the sink looked at me, then looked away quickly. I stayed on that bathroom floor until my legs stopped shaking enough to stand.

Back in my room, I spread the pamphlets out and stared at them.

Abortion. Prenatal care. Two paths.

I didn't know which one was right. I didn't know if either of them was right.

My phone was almost dead. Three percent battery. I should call Linda and ask for help.

But what would I say? That I'd gotten pregnant by a rapist? That I'd been drinking for six weeks straight? That I needed her to save me again?

She hung up on me last time. Told me she was done. I couldn't call her.

I walked to the plasma center. Maybe I could donate my blood and get forty dollars. Enough for food and another bottle.

But my hands were shaking too badly. The nurse took one look at me and said no, that I couldn't donate if I'd been drinking.

I tried the food bank, but they needed proof of residency. An ID with a local address. Mine still said Millfield.

"Come back when you have documentation," the woman said.

Every door slammed in my face. By the time the sun started setting, I was back at the liquor store, spending my last twelve dollars on vodka.

I walked to the church instead. The Catholic one with unlocked doors. Inside smelled like incense and old wood. It was empty except for me.

I sat in the back pew, staring at Jesus on the cross. Suffering for things he didn't do. Like this baby. Suffering for what someone did to me.

"It's not the baby's fault," I whispered.

The silence felt like it was crushing me.

I unscrewed the vodka and lifted it to my lips. Then I stopped and put the cap back on. My hands were shaking so hard the bottle rattled.

Six weeks. A heart beating somewhere inside me. Fighting to live while I fought to die.

I thought about Leo. How he'd called fourteen times asking for help. How I'd ignored every call.

This baby was calling for help too, in its own way. I could ignore it, like I ignored Leo, or I could answer.

I stood up, walked to the front of the church, found a trash can, and poured the vodka out, watching it splash into the garbage. Twelve dollars gone. My whole body started shaking harder. Withdrawal or fear, I couldn't tell.

A woman came through a side door. Older. Cleaning smock. She saw me and sat down in the pew next to me.

"You okay, honey?"

"No." The word came out broken.

"What do you need?"

"I don't know." Tears were running down my face now. "I don't know how to do this."

"Do what?"

"Any of it. All of it."

She was quiet for a minute. Then she said, "You know what helps me? One day at a time. Sometimes one hour. Just make it through right now."

"I can't."

"Just today. Can you make it through today?"

I thought about that. Just today. Twenty-four hours.

"Maybe," I whispered.

"Then that's enough." She patted my hand. "That's all God asks."

I walked back to the boarding house. My room was exactly as I'd left it: stained mattress, empty bottles everywhere.

I lay down and stared at the ceiling. My hands wouldn't stop shaking. My chest hurt. My whole body screamed for vodka. But I'd poured it out. It was gone.

I put my hands on my stomach. Still flat. Nothing showing.

"You're half him," I whispered. "Half monster. And I don't know if I can love you knowing that."

My throat closed up.

"I don't know if I can look at you and not see his face."

The truth of it felt like drowning.

"But maybe you're half me too. Half fighter."

I wiped my face with shaking hands.

"Maybe that's the half that matters."

I didn't sleep that night. I just lay there shaking, sweating through my clothes, my heart racing so fast I thought it would explode. Withdrawal felt like dying.

But I didn't drink.

Morning came. I was still shaking and still sweating, but alive.

Thirty-six hours sober. The longest I'd been in months.

I tried to eat. I bought a bagel from the gas station with the quarters I found in my pockets. I forced it down even though my stomach turned, even though food felt impossible.

The baby needed it. That thought kept coming back. The baby needs it. Even if I didn't want to eat. Even if I wanted to die. The baby needed me to live.

I walked to a payphone, put in my last quarters, and dialed Linda's number. She answered on the fourth ring. "Hello?"

Cautious. Tired.

"Mom, it's me."

Silence.

"Olivia."

Not a greeting. Just my name. Flat.

"I'm pregnant."

The silence stretched so long I thought she'd hung up.

"How far along?"

"Six weeks."

"Have you been drinking?"

"Yes. Every day. Until yesterday."

"Yesterday." Not a question. An accusation.

"I stopped yesterday. I'm trying to stop."

"Trying isn't the same as stopping, Olivia."

"I know." My voice cracked. "But I don't know how to do this. I don't know how to stop. I don't know how to be a mother. I just know I can't keep killing things."

Silence again. I could hear her breathing. Long and controlled, like she was making a decision.

"Come home."

The words were so quiet I almost didn't hear them.

"What?"

"Come home. Right now. Tonight."

"But you said you were done. You said—"

"I know what I said." Her voice was hard. Cold. "And I meant it. I'm done enabling you. Done watching you destroy yourself."

"Then why—"

"Because that baby didn't do anything wrong." Her voice shook. "And I won't punish my grandchild for your mistakes."

Grandchild. She'd said grandchild.

"But hear me clearly, Olivia. This is the last time. You drink once, you're gone. You lie once, you're gone. I'm doing this for that baby. Not for you."

The words should have hurt, but they felt fair.

"I understand."

"Do you have money for a bus ticket?"

"No."

She sighed. Long and tired. "What's the address? I'll send money. Western Union. You can pick it up in an hour."

"Mom—"

"Get on the next bus. Don't drink. Not one drop. Can you do that?"

I looked at my hands. Still shaking. My whole body screaming for vodka.

"I can try."

"Then try."

She hung up.

The bus pulled out of Cleveland at 11 PM. An hour to Mill-field.

I pressed my forehead against the cold window, watching the city lights fade behind me.

My hands were shaking. My stomach cramped. Sweat soaked through my shirt even though the bus was freezing.

Withdrawal felt like my body was eating itself from the inside.

A woman across the aisle kept looking at me. Concerned. Like she might ask if I was okay. I closed my eyes so she wouldn't.

I thought about Linda waiting at the bus station, about facing and trying to be sober, about being someone's mother and raising a child that was half me and half monster. I put my hands on my stomach.

"I don't know if I can do this," I whispered. So quiet nobody could hear. "I don't know if I can be what you need."

The baby didn't answer. Just kept growing and kept fighting. Like me. Still here despite everything that tried to kill me.

Maybe that was enough, and just trying was enough. Even if I failed and turned out to be exactly like Dad. At least I'd fail trying. That's more than I gave Leo.

The bus pulled into Millfield just after midnight. The parking lot was empty except for a few scattered cars, dark buildings, and streetlights casting yellow circles on wet pavement.

Linda was waiting in the parking lot, leaning against her car with her arms crossed.

She didn't hug me when I got off the bus. Didn't smile. Just looked at me with those tired eyes that had seen too much.

"You're sober?"

"Forty hours."

She picked up one of my garbage bags. "Then let's go home."

Not "welcome home," just "let's go."

Fair enough. I picked up the other bag and followed her to the car.

We drove in silence through the empty streets of Millfield, past the warehouse where they found Leo and the church where I'd broken down at his funeral. Past all the places I'd failed everyone I'd ever loved.

Linda pulled into her driveway, turned off the car, and sat there for a minute without moving.

"I can't go through this again," she said. Her voice was quiet, broken. "Watching someone I love destroy themselves. I did it with your father. I did it with Leo. I can't do it with you."

"I know."

"So if you're not serious about this... if you're just running home because you're scared... get back on that bus right now."

I looked at her. Really looked. She'd aged since I'd seen her last. More gray in her hair. More lines around her eyes. I'd done that. Me, Dad, and Leo. We'd worn her down to nothing.

"I'm serious," I said. "I don't know if I can do it, but I'm serious about trying."

She stared at me for a long time, searching my face for lies, for the same promises I'd broken before. Finally, she nodded.

We got out of the car. I followed her to the door with my garbage bags.

Linda opened it and stood aside to let me in. The house smelled the same: coffee and laundry detergent and home.

"Leo's room is ready," she said. "You can sleep there."

Leo's room, where he'd lived before the drugs took everything, where his drawings still hung on the walls.

Where I'd sleep now. In his space, taking what should've been his.

"Okay," I said.

Linda headed toward the kitchen, then stopped and turned back.

"Olivia?"

"Yeah?"

"I'm glad you called." Her voice was still guarded, still careful. "I'm glad you're trying."

She disappeared into the kitchen before I could answer.

I stood there in the doorway with my garbage bags. Forty hours sober. Six weeks pregnant. Homeless, broken, and terrified.

But home. I walked upstairs to Leo's room, put my bags down, and sat on his bed.

His drawings were still on the walls: superheroes, dragons, and worlds he'd imagined before reality crushed them.

I put my hands on my stomach.

"I'm going to try," I whispered. "I'm going to try to be better than him. Better than Dad. Better than all of them."

The baby didn't answer, just kept growing and fighting to exist.

Outside, the streetlights cast shadows across the front lawn. The house was quiet, dark except for the porch light Linda had left on.

I pulled the compass from my pocket. The one he gave me before he died, Grandpa's compass before that. I'd been carrying it since the bus station, holding onto it as if it could guide me.

I opened it. The needle swung back and forth, then settled, pointing north. North meant the right direction. The way forward.

I hoped keeping this baby was north. Hoped choosing to fight instead of run was north.

I didn't know for sure. Maybe I'd never know. But the needle was steady, and I'd made it through two days sober.

Tomorrow I'd try for three. One day at a time. That's all I could do. All anyone could do.

Try.

Chapter Thirteen

Author's Note

You've watched Olivia hit rock bottom. Fight for sobriety one brutal day at a time. Choose to keep a baby conceived in violence.

Books 1 and 2 were about survival. Books 3 through 5 are about what happens when survival isn't enough.

The man who raped her never faced charges. The system failed her. And now he wants custody of the daughter she fought so hard to save.

So Olivia makes a choice: she's going to fight back with the only weapons powerful people understand.

Money. Power. Their own game, played better than they ever expected.

These next three books shift into high gear: corporate warfare, calculated revenge, and a mother who refuses to lose.

Olivia doesn't abandon recovery. She weaponizes everything addiction tried to steal from her: her intelligence, her fury, her absolute refusal to quit.

The question is: How far would you go to protect your child?

Book 3: Blood Money starts with Olivia sober, her daughter alive, and her rapist walking free.

It doesn't end that way. Olivia's fight starts now. You can find Book 3 online, so don't wait. Just search ***"Blood Money by Howard Kane"*** wherever you buy books.

With gratitude,

Howard Kane

246

This page was intentionally left blank.

247

This page was intentionally left blank.

248

This page was intentionally left blank.

249

This page was intentionally left blank.

250

This page was intentionally left blank.